J.L. DAVIS

Meg-
enjoy!!!
♥
J.L. Davis
#Squad

Last

Published in the United States of America.

DEDICATION

This book is dedicated to the readers, for taking a chance on a new author. I hope you enjoy this story as much as I did writing it. Thanks so much!

PROLOGUE

When I was a little girl I would dream about what it would be like when I grew up. My dream was to have a job I loved, be respected and make a lot of money. I would have a big, beautiful house and a nice car. I pictured having a husband who was handsome and successful, and who treated me like a princess minus the crown. I guess that's why it was a dream, because my life is far from what I imagined. I wanted more for myself and the family I would have someday.

I was a high school dropout who moved in with my boyfriend Tyler. We lived in a small, one-bedroom apartment for about four years. I thought I was in love with him. For the most part, he treated me well.

One day, I came home early from my job working in a daycare because a toddler had puked all over me and it was even in my hair. Tyler was off that day so I was excited to shower and spend the afternoon with him. Only when I got home, I knew immediately something was off. I walked through the door and he wasn't sitting on the couch playing video games like he normally would be doing on his day off.

As I walked past our bedroom door I suddenly stopped. I could've sworn I heard noises coming from inside. When I open the door, he wasn't alone and what's worse is he was in bed with my best friend. My only friend. What the fuck?

I had been friends with Amber since the fifth grade. We were close or I thought we were anyway. I was so shocked. I got in my Honda Civic and drove to my mom's, even though we weren't on the best of terms. We'd stopped speaking for a while when I quit school and moved in with Tyler at seventeen.

I couldn't believe this shit. I had my whole life planned out I thought. I thought Tyler and I would get married and have a family and a happily ever after. I didn't think he would do something like that. Amber has always been kind of too friendly with guys, but I trusted her. I guess I should have read between the lines. She did flirt with him, but I thought it was in fun. I loved Tyler, but maybe I wasn't in love with him. This proved that to be true because I wasn't heartbroken like I thought I should have been.

I went back a few days later when I knew Tyler wouldn't be home and packed my shit. I didn't have too much and was glad because I didn't want to be there any longer than I had to be. When I walked in what was our bedroom and looked at the bed I was livid. I trashed it on my way out and felt better about it than I should have. I had gotten a little closure, I guess. Tyler was never worthy of my trust, loyalty and definitely not my love. I decided that that was the last time I will be so stupid when it came to a man.

CHAPTER ONE

So here I am: Jessa Phillips, twenty-one, without a boyfriend, or best friend, and living with my mom again. Oh, and let's not forget, jobless since my previous employer was Tyler's mother and there was no way in hell I'd be stepping foot in her smelly daycare ever again.

After a couple of depressing weeks and feeling sorry for myself I needed to seriously start looking for a job. Since I am a dropout and don't have any other talents or a resume, my options are very limited. I love reading a good steamy romance, cleaning, organizing, and of course taking care of children. Though, I really don't want to do that anymore if I didn't have to.

I give up and go to the kitchen, grab some Oreo cookies and going to the bay window to watch the world go by. As I finish the bag I see a woman pull up across the street. She gets out of her sky-blue Prius to go to her trunk and pulls out a bucket and a mop. As she lowers her trunk she spots me in the window watching her and waves with a big smile. That's when it hit me. I love to clean, so maybe I can clean people's houses, too! I run upstairs to my mom's office and google house cleaning.

I learn that depending on what the house cleaner is willing to do, housekeeping can be a great money maker. I print out some flyers and get dressed. I drive into town and leave flyers at a few places I think will be beneficial, the grocery store, flower shop, dry cleaners, pharmacy, and the last one at the bank. I'm putting the last tack in when I hear my name. I turn around and see a girl I went to high school with. I think her name is Brittany. She's just as beautiful as she was in school. I take a quick notice, she's dressed professionally. Looks like she's doing well for herself.

"Hi! Jessa, it's been forever. How are you?"

I slightly cringe, "I've been better but hopefully things will get better soon." I plaster on a fake smile, hoping she will believe it, even if I don't. I move to block the board that has my flyer pinned on it. I don't want her to see it. I'm embarrassed. I shouldn't be, but I am.

She looks at the bulletin and I see her looking at my flyer.

"Jessa are you starting your own business?"

I didn't think of it that way, but I guess I am.

"Yeah. I decided I needed a fresh start and wanted to try something new."

"That's awesome! I actually know someone who needs help," she says smiling, not at all looking down on my new profession.

"Okay, that'll be great," I smile.

"I will! It was so good to see you. We should get drinks sometime real soon."

"That sounds great," I say as we walked out to our cars.

"I'm serious about those drinks, Jessa. I'd love to catch up."

"Definitely. You have my number. Text me yours."

She smiles and gets in her shiny car and drives away.

The next morning, I shower and dress for the day. I have a text from a number I don't recognize. I open it.

Hi! This is Alex Rogan. My niece, Brittany gave me your number. I'm very interested in your services.

Hi! This is Jessa. Thank you for taking an interest in my services. How many square feet is the house and when is a good time to come look at it?

His reply is almost instantly.

The house is about 4,500 square feet. I'm free tonight if you'd like to come look at it and give me a price? I know it's short notice and I understand if you already have plans. I'm usually here so I'm sure we can find a time to meet.

It's a big house. I didn't really think about cleaning a house that size. My mom's house is about 2,000 square feet and it takes me about three hours to clean it, if I don't get sidetracked organizing.

Tonight, will be great. I didn't have any plans. How about 6:00?

I think of how pathetic I probably am, not having plans on a Friday night. My phone beeps again with his reply.

6:00 will be perfect. I look forward to it.

I try not to think about being held in the basement. I'm sure that's where his wife keeps her big wine assortment. That thought makes me laugh. It will be fine.

—

At five thirty I'm ready to go look at the house. I get in my old Honda Civic and put the address in my GPS on my phone. I should arrive a few minutes early it looks like.

I pull up to a house that's in a gated community. I'm so out of my element here. It is in fact huge and beautiful. It's a grey, two-story brick home with bright white painted shutters. The landscaping is perfect. There are hydrangeas that wrap around the porch. His wife has wonderful taste. Hydrangeas are my favorite flower. I absolutely love this place.

As I walk up the sidewalk in my normal clothes and Converse I start to feel extremely out of place. Maybe I should've worn something nicer, and not an old pair of jeans with a hole in them. I sigh, take a deep breath and ring the doorbell. A few seconds later the door opens and what I see is nothing like I imagined. He's six foot or maybe a bit taller. He has light brown hair and the lightest blue eyes I've ever seen. They remind me of the ocean. You can see right through them. He looks freshly shaven with the cutest dimples when he smiles down a me. He looks me over in a way that makes me uncomfortable but also makes my heart speed up a bit. I may be a bit aroused. I'm an average girl, about five-foot-three. Nothing too special. I have dark brown hair and eyes and don't eat right. Everyone's always told me I'm lucky to have such a high metabolism. I don't work out. He does for sure. He looks like he's never missed a gym day in his life. I want to run my hands over his strong arms that fill out his shirt perfectly.

I didn't realize until now that we are staring at each other. I shift my eyes and he clears his throat to speak.

"Jessa, it's nice to meet you. Please come in."

I walk in and it's quiet. I don't think anyone else is here. I hear the door close and a sigh from Alex. He clears his throat again and walks up beside me. I wonder if he clears his throat when he's nervous?

"I hope I'm not keeping you from anything tonight by

coming here to meet?"

"No, not at all." I try to keep my voice level and not give away my nervousness.

"I've never done this before but I'm guessing you want the tour?" He's smiling at me and my heart melts. He has an amazing smile with beautiful white teeth.

"Lead the way," I smile.

I follow him through each room and can't help but look at his ass. It fills his jeans perfectly. I wonder how firm it is? Focus, Jessa! He leads us upstairs and I see a few guest rooms and bathrooms. He passes a couple of doors that must be closets. He opens a set of double doors and allows me inside. It's the master bedroom. He follows behind me. It's a beautiful bedroom. There's a king size bed with a bunch of pillows pushed to one side that hasn't been touched. I wonder if he lives in this huge house alone? I continue the tour walking into the master bathroom.

"Wow! This is beautiful."

"Thank you."

There's a huge walk-in shower, Jacuzzi tub, and matching his and her sinks. I notice his side has a toothbrush and some other things, but the other side is bare. I'm starting to think he does live here alone, but I am not going to question it. I turn around to walk out. I notice him standing at the door watching me. I don't know what I should do, so I just walk towards the door. He lets me by and he follows. We go back downstairs, and I can breathe again. I walk into the massive kitchen and sit at the table. He sits across from me.

"Mr. Rogan, I have a few questions, and then I can give you a price."

"Please, call me Alex," he says with a smile. Ugh, that smile. I'm going to melt on these beautiful marble floors.

"How many people live in the house?" I need to know this, but also want to know for myself.

"Just me," he says and I can hear sadness in his answer.

"Do you need me to do laundry and change sheets?"

"That would be great," he says a little too happy. I laugh because most men hate doing laundry.

I ask a few more questions and give the list of what I offer. I can think of something else I could offer, but that's not in the job description, sadly.

"It will definitely take me a few hours to do everything. I shouldn't need to hit every room each time, with just you here." I feel kind of bad saying that, but it's true. "How often do you want me to come?"

"Well, I'm a bit OCD and was thinking maybe Monday and Thursday each week, that's if you're able to?"

"Sure. I can do that. No problem at all." I could almost jump on him. A man who's hot as fuck and likes clean spaces. How is he even single? "What would be a good time, so I'm not in the way of you getting ready for work?"

"I work from home, actually. I own a construction company and can do most of my work from here. My assistant comes by a lot. She's also my niece and loves the pool," he smiles. "She gave me your number."

"Oh, Brittany. We went to school together."

We look at each other a bit too long and he clears his throat. That is definitely a nervous habit. I think it's cute. Everyone has one.

He pulls me out of my thoughts, "Jessa how much do you think it will cost for you to work for me?"

"I think one hundred dollars will cover everything we've discussed." He immediately shakes his head. I'm mortified. He thinks it's too much.

"Jessa, that's not enough. For your time and gas twice a week I think one hundred and forty is much more appropriate." I must look ridiculous staring at him with wide eyes. He laughs.

I stand, "Thank you." He stands and holds a hand out. I grab it and instantly feel the sparks. He looks at me and pulls away quickly. He felt it, too. I've never felt it. I've only read about it in books. I quickly say, "Is eight okay to come?" Kill me now.

"That will be perfect. I get back from the gym around seven forty-five," he says as we walk to the door.

"Of course you do." He smiles and I realize I said that shit out loud. I'm so fucking embarrassed right now. I could die.

"It was so nice to meet you Jessa and I'll see you Monday." He's still smiling.

"Bye," is all I can manage. I walk to my car quickly. I

swear I see him watching from the window. I take a deep breath, start my car and drive away.

CHAPTER TWO

I make it home and turn my car off and sit there for a few minutes going over the meeting with Alex in my head. I can't believe how fucking gorgeous he is. I kind of got the feeling he was nervous, too, and a little uncomfortable with me being there. He wants me to clean for him so he should be able to trust me being there. Maybe he just needs to get used to the idea. I know I do. I still don't quite understand why he lives in such a big house alone. I'm not going to overthink it anymore. I am happy to have this job. I don't have much left in savings.

I go inside and make a list of what all I will need to start my new job, but I can't stop thinking about Alex. From what I'd seen, he seemed nice and it makes me wonder what flaws he has besides being OCD. In my book that is a great quality to have. I'm a bit OCD myself. I suppose is a good thing since I'll be cleaning his house.

I take a shower and get comfy in my bed. I lie awake thinking of Alex. That spark when he held my hand, I just can't quit thinking about it. I know he must have felt it, too. I've never felt that before. I'd read about it and wondered what that would feel like. I can't get him out of my head. I can feel my clit throbbing and my panties getting wet just thinking about his eyes and his mouth and his body. I want to feel him kissing and touching me. I reach under my bed and grab Bob, my battery-operated boyfriend. He's pretty awesome, but definitely not the real thing. I lay back, close my eyes and think of Alex as I reach into my panties and rub Bob over my clit and down to the wetness and back up again. I imagine him spreading my legs holding me in place and his mouth clamping down over my clit, him flicking his tongue as he sucked hard. I'm so turned on and wet I can hardly keep Bob in my hand. I can feel my orgasm building. My legs begin to shake and my breathing becomes labored. I bite my lower lip thinking of Alex biting me to quiet my moans. My back arches off the bed and my orgasm crashes through me. I lay there a few minutes to catch my breath and gain the feeling back in my legs and go to the bathroom to wash up. I get back in bed relaxed and drift off to sleep.

The rest of the weekend flies by. I sit around reading a good romance book and go to the store to pick up my supplies for tomorrow. I'm excited and nervous about this new chapter of my life. When I get home my mom is here. I grab my bags and hurry inside to tell her all about it.

"Mom, I have a job. I start tomorrow, cleaning a house twice a week."

"That's great, honey. I want you to also look this over." She hands me a packet that's for the GED class in town. I really do need to take it. I don't want to clean houses for the rest of my life. I'm happy to have this new job, but I want something to be proud of.

"Thanks. I'll look it over and find time to do it. I know I disappointed you by quitting school and moving in with Tyler. That was a huge mistake. I realize that now."

"Jessa, you know I love you and everyone makes bad decisions in life. Your father was mine," she smiles. They had a horrible marriage. Mom stayed with him to keep me from being part of a broken home. Eventually she'd had enough and they divorced when I was twelve. We haven't seen him since. I don't understand how a father could leave his child like that. I don't know if he's even alive. I try not to think about him. It just pisses me off.

"I love you, too, mom and I'm so grateful for you letting me move back in."

She orders our favorite Chinese for supper. She stays with her boyfriend, Edward, a lot but we try to have dinner together once a week to catch up. As we eat, I tell her a little about Alex's house, but I don't tell her anything about him, especially how hot he is. She tells me about her weekend with Edward. Before she gets into graphic details of the night I say goodnight and hurry to bed to be ready for tomorrow. She tends to overshare and I don't want nightmares of what Edward does to her in bed. I don't need those images before going to sleep.

I lay here thinking about how my life has changed over

the last few months. I think about Alex and his life story. How he has his own business and live in that big house all alone? If I had to guess, he might be thirty and to be so successful is amazing. I hope I can work around him and not be nervous. He's just a man I'm working for. He's a sexy as fuck man, but I should be able to stay professional and hopefully he doesn't catch me staring.

—

My alarm goes off at six thirty. I'm excited to have a purpose, but also, nervous to see him again. I throw on a t-shirt, jeans and my favorite Converse. I put my hair in a messy bun and brush my teeth. Should I put on some makeup? Hell no! I'm cleaning his house not trying to impress him. Am I? I need to stop thinking so much. I'm working for him, not going to bed with him. Unfortunately, that's not happening.

I walk downstairs and grab all my supplies and get ready to leave. I put everything in my trunk and go back inside for my coffee and lunch.

"I'm leaving," I yell out to my mom.

"Have a great first day," she yells down.

I head back out the door and get in my car. I turn the key and... nothing. I hear a clicking sound. What the fuck? I don't need this on my first day. I hurry back in as mom's coming down the stairs.

"What's wrong honey?"

"I think my battery's dead. Can you drop me off on your

way to work?"

"Sure, give me a few more minutes and we can leave."

"Thanks, mom." I hurry outside and put all my stuff in the back of her SUV. She comes out and we leave. I give her the address and notice she's impressed. I didn't tell her anything about Alex on the way there. She's a bit nosy and would have too many questions. Most I probably wouldn't have answers to give anyway.

We pull up and she sees the house. "Jessa you better be careful not to break anything," she smiles at me.

"Always the joker mom."

She kisses my cheek. "I love you and good luck today."

"Thanks, mom. I love you, too."

"Let me know if you'll need a ride home."

"Okay. I'm not sure how long I'll be here, but I'll let you know."

I smile and close the door and get my stuff out the back and she drives away.

I walk up to the door, take a few deep breaths and ring the doorbell. My heart is pounding out of my chest. Why am I so nervous? Alex is only a man, a drop dead gorgeous man, but none the less, just a man. He opens the door and smiles. I could faint right now. He's not wearing a shirt. My eyes fall to his chest and he has an amazing six pack and, oh God, he has the V that leads to a magical place. The V makes girls stupid. He clears his throat and I realize I've been staring. I feel my face heat. Stupid face. It always gives me away. I wish

I wasn't this affected by him.

He smiles. "I wasn't sure if you were coming. I was about to jump in the shower."

Really! Really! Why is he torturing me like this? He must know what he's doing and how he's affecting me.

"I'm on time," I smile.

He looks at his smart watch. "So you are. Come in. It's a bit chilly today."

He's making small talk. I can play along. I walk in, "It is and tomorrow will probably feel like summer."

He laughs. "Yes Arkansas is very unpredictable." He steps aside so I can go inside.

"Where do you want me? I mean to start?"

"I'll go upstairs and shower and then be in my office working. Wherever you'd like," he says gesturing around the house.

"I'll start upstairs and work my way down, then."

"Sounds great," he smiles and heads up the stairs.

I start in a guestroom far away from him in the shower. I'd love to see what he looks like with the water falling all over his body, but who am I kidding? I could never sneak a peek. I finish the guest rooms and the connecting bathrooms. They are hardly used and easy to clean. I don't understand why he wants me here twice a week. I almost feel like I'm taking advantage. I may need to talk with him about this if it's always this easy.

I walk into the next open door and I don't remember

this one the other day. It's a massive library with a reading nook in the corner. I run my hand across a few titles. I have some of these. They're all romance and erotica novels. Why would he have all of these? He didn't show me this room. I would've remembered. I'm in heaven. The doorbell rings and I can hear the shower is still on so I hurry down the stairs. I open the door and Brittany is standing there.

"Jessa! Hi! I'm so glad it worked out for you to work for Alex," she smiles looking beautiful in her button up shirt and skirt while I stand here in jeans and a plain shirt.

"Hi!" I step aside and let her in.

"Where's Alex?"

"He's upstairs in the shower. He should be finished soon."

"Okay. I have some papers he needs to sign. I'll wait in the living room."

She sits on the couch and turns on the tv. "So, how do you like working here so far?"

"It's my first day and it's going pretty well."

"Good. Do you want to go out for drinks later and catch up? It's been a while. I missed you when you didn't come back to school."

"Yeah, that sounds great. I made some horrible choices, didn't I?"

"Hey, guys can make us stupid sometimes."

"That's for damn sure," I laugh. "I'm going to get back to work, but I'll call you after I leave and we can get together."

"Awesome!"

I go back up the stairs and can smell Alex's body wash, it's intoxicating. He walks out of the master pulling his shirt over his head. It's almost a disappointment, but I don't need the distraction.

"Brittany is downstairs waiting for you."

"Okay, thanks," he smiles down at me. He's so much taller than I am.

"Are you finished in there," I nod to the master bedroom.

"Yes. It's all yours."

I smile and walk towards the door. Entering the bathroom, I immediately start sliding across the floor. I scream and hit the floor. Oh, my ass. Alex comes running into the bathroom.

"Oh no, Jessa. Are you alright? I'm so sorry."

"I think so." I can't look at him. I'm too embarrassed. He has his arm around my waist trying to help me up and I wince. My ass hurts but the pounding in my chest has more of my attention now because he's holding me. He's searching my face to be sure I'm okay. Our eyes lock at that moment. I'm not sure, but it seems like he may kiss me. I want him to. Brittany walks in at that moment, "Is everything.... oh, am I interrupting something?" Alex scowls at her letting go of my waist. I suppose he was just concerned and wasn't going to kiss me. I guess I'll never know.

"I slipped and fell on the wet floor," I say, finally standing up.

"Are you sure you're okay," Alex asks again.

"Yes. I think I'm okay."

"If you need anything we'll be downstairs."

"Okay. Thank you." I'll be okay. My ego is just as bruised as my ass will be.

I finish upstairs and busy myself downstairs. I haven't seen Alex or Brittany since my big fall. They must be in his office. The door is closed and I can hear them talking, but it's muffled and I won't bother them. I put a load of laundry in the dryer. He is a boxer guy. I almost want to sneak a pair home with me but that would be too weird and a bit psycho. I walk in the kitchen as Brittany and Alex exit the office.

"Jessa, where is your car?" Brittany asks.

"My battery died so I had my mom drop me off." How embarrassing and pathetic. I feel my face heating.

"Oh, okay. I'll take you home and then we can go out later if you're okay?"

"That sounds great. I'm almost finished here."

"Do you need a new battery or maybe just a charge?" Alex asks.

"I'm not sure, really. I think we have a charger, but I don't really know how to hook it up."

"I could come by and look at it for you, if you want?"

"That's awfully nice of you, but I couldn't ask you to do that."

"Jessa, it's really no bother at all," he smiles at me.

Brittany is watching him with a grin on her face and I don't understand why.

"If you really are sure, that would be great. I don't have anyone to help me with it."

"No problem at all. I can come by later this afternoon on my way back from a job site. Write your address down for me before you leave."

"Okay. Thanks so much!"

I finish up for the day. Brittany hung around until I finished to drop me off at home.

I walk to Alex's office and knock on the door. "Come in." I walk in and he looks up from his desk and smiles. "Are you finished?"

"I am. Do you want to take look around?"

"No need. I looked a bit earlier." He stands and walks toward me. "I'll write you a check. Again, I'm so sorry that you fell. I hope you're gonna be okay," he says, walking to the kitchen. I follow, enjoying the view in front of me.

"I'll be fine," I smile shyly, standing at the counter. "I guess I should have worn different shoes."

Alex laughs. "You're probably right." I catch him look over me down to my feet.

"Are you ready, Jessa?" Brittany asks, entering the kitchen looking at her uncle.

"Yes. I am." Alex hands me my check and smiles.

"Thanks again, Jessa. The house looks great."

"Thank you. Same time Thursday?"

"Yep. I'll look forward to it," he says, walking us to the door.

"Bye, Alex," we say in unison laughing at each other.

"Bye girls," he laughs.

CHAPTER THREE

Brittany and I get in her two-door Mercedes. It's white with a black leather interior. Alex must pay her well to have this car. When we leave, it purrs like a kitten and picks up speed quickly. That's something I'm not used to in my old, 90's model Honda Civic. It gets me where I need to go, so that's all I care about.

"So, what did you think of Alex?" She looks at me grinning like a school girl.

I look at her and smile. "You could've warned me about how hot he is."

"Gross, Jessa. He's my uncle." I laugh at her.

"Sorry, but when he answered the door without a shirt on I thought I was going to die."

"He did not!" She's shocked and cracks up laughing. "He so did," I counter giggling.

"So, where do you want to go for dinner and drinks?" she asks.

"I'm pretty easy. You pick. I can't wait to catch up more. I haven't done anything fun lately. I've been depressed about everything. Not exactly how I thought my life was heading.

Ya know?"

"Well, I'll help fix that," she smiles. "What do you like to do?"

"I read a lot of romance and erotica novels."

"Oh yeah? Me too! We'll have to compare some that we've read."

"Okay. I have a few favorites I would recommend."

"What kind of music do like now?" she asks.

"Pretty much anything except country. It's depressing."

"I so agree. I'm not a big fan, either. Have you been to the new pub in town? They don't play any country."

"I went a couple times with Tyler," I say, rolling my eyes.

"Oh! Do you want to go somewhere else?"

"Nah. He probably can't afford to go anywhere anymore," I laugh.

We pull up to my mom's and Brittany turns the car off turning to face me, "Okay. So, you're good with going to the pub?"

"Sure. I'm good with it. I'm excited to do something fun and hang with you."

"Awesome! Me too. Is eight okay to meet there?"

"That's perfect. It gives me time to get ready and for Alex to look at my battery. Thanks so much for bringing me home."

"No problem at all. I'll see you later. Don't have too much fun with Alex," she laughs as she drives away.

I walk inside and head straight for the bathroom to see how badly my ass is bruised. I bruise so easily and was pretty sure my tail bone would be black and blue by now. When I pull my jeans down, it is in fact bruising and sore. I turn the water on for a bath and put lavender Epsom salts in to help ease the pain. I soak for quite a while, until my hands turn into prunes. As I get out and grab a towel, the doorbell rings. Shit! It must be Alex. I should get dressed, but I want to give him a taste of his own medicine. He answered his door half naked so I think I will do the same. I quickly wrap the towel around myself and hurry downstairs to answer the door.

As I open the door, he's drinking from a water bottle. When he sees me standing there he starts choking and coughing. He wasn't expecting me to dish it back to him by answering the door in my towel. "Are you alright," I ask concerned. I'm thrilled inside.

He's trying to catch his breath and manages a strangled "Uh, yeah, I'm fine." He looks over my body and I can feel my nipples peak through my towel. "Would you like to come in so the whole neighborhood doesn't see me in my towel?"

"Yeah, sure. Sorry." He walks in and I close the door. I want to laugh so hard right now.

I turn back around and look at him, he's staring at me again. I must admit, I am enjoying how I'm affecting him.

"I'm gonna go get dressed really quick and I'll be right back down. You can sit in the living room if you want." I point to the couch and hurry upstairs, gripping my towel so

I don't lose it.

I put on a tank top and shorts. When I make it back downstairs he's looking at photos of my mom and I above the fireplace.

"Sorry, I didn't expect you so soon."

He turns around and has a strange look on his face. "Is this your mom?" Pointing to one of the pictures.

"Yes. Please don't say we look alike. I hear it all the time."

He quickly changes the subject. "Can you show me where the battery charger is?"

"Sure. It's in the garage, I believe." He follows behind me. I turn around to switch the light on and run right into his rock, hard chest. I didn't know he was that close behind me. He smells so good and I breathe him in. He looks down at me as I look up at him, our eyes meet and he quickly looks away. I step back quickly, embarrassed that he didn't make a move. I'm disappointed because I think I wanted him to. I turn the light on and we walk in. I hand him the charger and follow him back outside to my car. I don't know if I did something wrong but he's acting strange now. He hooks it up quickly and looks at me, "It should take a few hours to charge, then you can remove the cables and you should be good to go."

"Okay. Thank you for helping me."

"No. problem. I'll see you later." He gets in his truck and drives away.

I arrive about ten minutes early. It is a nice pub/bar. It's the best of both. It has really good food and drinks, a few pool tables, and a small dance floor in the corner. I sit at the far side of the bar so I can see who walks in. I like to people watch.

"What can I get you, pretty lady?" the bartender asks me. I look over the menu and finally decide.

"I'll have an apple crown and cranberry on the rocks please," handing him the menu.

"Coming right up," he slaps the bar and walks away busying himself with my drink. I watch him as he makes it. He is cute. He has a tattoo on his forearm. I can't quite make it out. He brings me my drink and sets it down with a napkin. "Let me know if you need anything else," he says, smiling at me.

"I will. Thank you," I smile and he walks away to tend to another customer.

Brittany arrives a few minutes later and wastes no time. She orders us each a shot of tequila. I'm not a big fan, but I humor her. It goes down and burns my throat, hitting rock bottom in my stomach. I'm going to need food soon if she keeps this up.

"Sorry I'm late. I had to run some papers over to Alex."

"It's okay. I was just watching the cute bartender," nodding towards him.

"You look cute," she says.

"Thanks. You're not used to seeing me all dressed up," I say, wiggling my eyebrows at her.

She's staring at me and it's kind of weird. "What?"

"Nothing. You just remind me of someone."

"Oh, okay. I thought maybe I had a booger or something." I laugh.

Brittany flags the bartender. "Can we have another round please?"

"If I keep having tequila I'm going to need some food in my stomach very soon."

"Okay. Let's eat and then go dance it off."

"That sounds great!"

We share some cheese fries and have more shots. We are both pretty tipsy now. We walk on to the dance floor. There's pop music playing and I see there are a few others also dancing. There's a few strobe lights for effect. My favorite song comes on over the sound system and I start dancing beside Brittany. We are having a great time together, so far. A guy comes dancing between us, wanting our attention. I look him over. He is cute, but by the look of his hair I'm betting he takes longer than I do to get ready. I'm not into pretty boys. I like manly men. I try to get closer to Brittany so maybe he'll get the point and go away, but no such luck. We look at each other and smile. "More drinks?"

I nod my head quickly, "Yes!"

We stand at the bar and the bartender walks over smiling, "Same?"

"Yes. Please," I smile back.

He returns with our drinks. We raise our shots and sling them back. That one wasn't bad at all. That must mean we're almost drunk. "I need to walk around," I admit.

"How about some pool?" Brittany asks.

"Okay. I'm not very good but I like to play," I laugh.

We find an open table and I rack the balls. Well, I try to. We pick our sticks out and Brittany breaks. We each try getting our balls in; this will be long game. We both suck. It's pretty funny, actually.

"I fucking suck!" Brittany yells. "I gotta go pee. I'll be right back."

I nod and laugh at her as she hurries to the bathroom. I bend down on the table with my stick to see how I can make my shot. One of Brittany's balls is in the way of me sinking the eight ball in the corner pocket for the win. I'm contemplating how I can do it.

"You're holding the stick wrong." I jump. Holy shit. I'd recognize that sexy voice anywhere. I'm a little drunk and I don't want him to see me like this. I turn around, not realizing how close he is to me and he smiles knowing he startled me. Ugh! When he smiles I just become a puddle in the floor. I decide I can play with him a bit too. I've had a bit of liquid courage.

"Wanna show me how to hold it?" He can take that however he wants. I may have the courage but my face still heats. He takes it exactly how I meant it. His smile disappears and I see his eyes darken.

"Bend over and I'll show you." I immediately turn around facing the table; I don't want him to see me blushing. I bend over the table. He's very close behind me and puts his arms around me, maneuvering my pool stick between my fingers. The heat from his body and the smell of his cologne is intoxicating and almost too much for me to handle. My heart is racing.

"Make sure to have your right hand further back on the stick so you have more control of where you're trying to make the ball go. Does that make sense?"

When he speaks, he's so close to my ear it causes me to shiver and I feel goosebumps rise on the back of my neck. I'm trying to concentrate, but he's so distracting.

"Yes. I think so. I'm not very good," I laugh.

I'm trying to concentrate. I feel him step back just as Brittany walks up to the table. I aim and make the eight ball in the corner pocket. I scream with excitement, jumping into his arms. Alex smiles but I don't think he knows what to think about my arms wrapped around him.

"I'm sorry. I shouldn't have done that," I say, letting go of him quickly.

"It's okay," he says grinning.

"Alex why are you here?" Brittany asks annoyed. "If I'd known you were coming you could've saved myself the trip to your house."

"I finished and thought I'd come out for a bit. I thought

you girls may need someone to look after you," he smiles.

"That was sweet of you," she says sarcastically, frowning at him.

"Jessa since you beat me you can buy the next round," she laughs.

"Uh, I'm not sure that's how that works," I say, giggling as we all walk to the bar.

It's close to eleven thirty now and I need to eat something. I'm hoping it will help sober me up. I've drank too much and don't know if I'll be able to drive myself home. Brittany is quite tipsy, also. The waitress comes over, "What can I get y'all?" She's talking to all of us but her eyes are only on Alex. I guess he has that effect on all women. I don't blame her at all. I feel the same way.

"I'll have a water and some nachos, please," I say and she writes it down, but her eyes never leave Alex. I want to slap her.

"I'll have the same," Brittany says, looking at me rolling her eyes. "Um, did you get that or are you gonna stare all night?"

I bust out laughing and I can't believe she just said that, but I want to high five her.

She ignores Brittany's comment, "What would you like, handsome?"

Alex taps his fingers on the table trying to decide. "Make that three." I look over at him and he isn't acknowledging her at all. He's looking at me. I smile and look up at the waitress as she walks away unhappy. I hope she doesn't spit in our nachos.

We eat our nachos and drink our waters and don't have any more issues with the waitress other than seeing glance over at Alex a few more times.

"So do y'all think you'll be able to drive home?" Alex asks, looking at Brittany and I. Brittany looks at me crazy and we both laugh.

"Honestly, I don't think we can," she says to her uncle. He rolls his eyes and shakes his head.

"I thought as much. Come on I'll take you both home," getting up from the table and leaving a few bills to cover the bill.

"Alex, I can pay for my food," I say.

He looks at me like I'm crazy. "You will not."

I stand and I see his eyes looking over my body and it excites me. "Thank you," I say as I walk towards him. Brittany follows and we walk out like the three musketeers. Alex drapes his arms around us as we walk to his truck. It has been a great night. I needed to have some fun, and when Alex joined us it made it that much better.

CHAPTER FIVE

The next morning, I feel like shit. My head is pounding. I had every intention of getting up early and going to take the GED test. I get up and call to see when the next scheduled time is and there's another at noon. I have a couple of hours to get ready and look over a few math problems that could possibly be on the test. I'm confident I can pass. I was smart in school, when I went.

I walk through the door and sign in. In the room, I take a seat at one of the desks. There are a few others here, also. I look around the room and see a girl that's maybe twenty sitting a couple of seats down and she smiles at me. I smile and tap my foot impatiently. I'm ready to get this over with and behind me.

A man in his mid-forties walks in with a briefcase and takes a seat at the front of the class. He must be the instructor. He smiles. "Welcome to the class. I will need everyone to turn all cell phones off and put them away and then I will distribute the tests. You'll have three hours to complete and return the test to me. I will then drop them off and your grades will be posted on the website within seventy-two hours. I need everyone to set up an ID and password to enter the site. I will give you the ID number as you return your test. Does anyone have any questions before we begin?" He looks around the room as does everyone else. "Alright I will now pass out the tests and you may begin."

I think I did well. My only issues were a few math equations. If those are the only ones I got wrong, then I should be fine. Now the waiting. I am ready to get my results so I can enroll into a tech-college online. I want to go into business. There are several jobs that qualify with a business degree. There are a few eight-week courses to get me started. If I decide to go further, then I will.

I pull into the driveway and receive a text from Brittany.

I feel like shit. How about you?

Same.

Do you want to get some coffee? I'm about to leave the office for a bit.

Sure. Starbucks?

Yes. I'll be there in ten.

Ok. See you there.

Being a small town, we were lucky to recently get a Starbucks. There's been several new businesses going up the last few years, and the population has slowly been growing.

I walk in and the smell is heaven. I could live here, it smells so good. I see Brittany seated in a corner with her coffee and laptop, typing away. I walk up to the counter and wait for the barista to take my order. "Hi! Welcome to Starbucks. What can I get started for you?" He's smiling and is very handsome. There are always cute college guys working at Starbucks. I haven't been to one where there isn't.

"I'll have a venti, mocha frappuccino with no whip, please," I smile.

"A lady who knows what she wants," he says as I step aside. I think about what he'd just said. I do know what I want, but can't have it.

"Here you go," he says, pulling me from my thoughts. "That will be $5.83."

I reach in my purse pulling out a five and a couple of ones. "Keep the change," I smile and walk to the table where Brittany is still working.

"Hi!" I say, taking the seat across from her.

"Hey, sorry, give me one minute and I'll be finished." She types a bit more and closes her laptop. "Okay. So, you feel like shit too, huh?"

"Yes. I should get something to eat and maybe that will help. Do you want anything?"

"Nah. I'm good. I had a muffin when I first got here."

"Okay, I'm going to order a panini. The new chicken one sounds delicious."

I return to the table and waste no time diving in. The only thing I had yesterday were the nachos late last night. I take a bite and moan my appreciation for the flaky goodness. It is good. I know I'm starved, but this may be my new favorite.

"So, there's a local band playing at the club tomorrow night." Brittany says, almost ready to bounce out of her seat.

"Oh yeah," I giggle.

"Yes, they're really good and super fuckable in the looks department. It won't take long for them to hit it big. Do you want to come with?"

"Sounds fun. What time?"

"I think eight. We could get there a little early and eat first, so we don't have a repeat of last night," she winces. "How about seven?"

"Sounds good to me."

"My brother, Nick, will be coming along too. He's friends with the drummer," she says, rolling her eyes and I nod. I don't remember her brother much. I think he was a couple of years older than us.

Wednesday evening comes fast. I'm excited about the show. I shower and shave and am now standing in my towel looking in my closet for something to wear. I try on a dozen different outfits, tossing them to the floor in frustration as I take them off. I have no clue what to wear, not happy with anything I've tried so far. In the very back of my closet I find a little black dress that I ordered online a couple of years ago. It was a little bit too big and I couldn't return it. I snatch it from the hanger and try it on. Holy shit! It fits. I turn and look over myself. I've gained a few pounds in the last couple of years. Fast food will do that to you. It fits great. I grab a strappy pair of heels, nothing too high. I'd break an ankle. I don't know how girls can wear stilettos, makes my feet hurt just seeing someone walking in them. I walk back in the bathroom and put on a little makeup. I look at my reflection in the mirror happy that my eyelashes look good on both eyes. I swear, one eye always clumps and the other looks perfect. On the way, out of the bathroom I spray some perfume on and grab my wristlet.

I arrive at seven. There parking lot is almost full. I guess they do put on a good show. I find a spot all the way in the back. I reach the door and a big, bulky bald man is standing there to check my ID and take my cover charge. He looks down my body, "Have a good night." I hurry inside.

I stop just inside the entrance and search through the massive crowd for Brittany. I finally spot her near the bar talking to a hot, tall, blonde haired guy. I walk towards them and Brittany spots me and smiles. I hug her and she nods to the hot guy. "This is my older, but not smarter, brother,

Nick," she smiles, joking with him and he rolls his eyes. I find myself looking him over. He is wearing a black shirt that hugs his biceps. He has beautiful, light brown eyes with what I believe are hints of green around the edges. It's hard to tell with the lighting.

"Where have you been hiding?" he asks, as his eyes are looking at my chest and down my body.

"Huh? What do you mean?" I'm confused.

Brittany chimes in just then, sounding a bit irritated, "That's his way of hitting on you," she sighs. I can't help it. I start laughing because that was not a good line. He looks at me a little shocked, maybe a little embarrassed.

"I'm sorry to laugh." I shake my head, still giggling. He smiles at me and I finally gain my composure. A beautiful waitress comes up. She's wearing a very tiny tank top with even tinier shorts that shows off the many tattoos on her body. I don't blame her. She needs her tips. Her boobs are huge and Nick takes notice immediately. "What can I get you?" She's looking at me as if she's undressing me with her eyes. I'm a little thrown. I just assumed she'd be bending over backwards for Nick, the hot guy standing next to me.

"Um," Brittany jumps in, "we'll have three shots of tequila." She wraps her arms around me. The waitress says nothing and leaves quickly to get our order. "Oh my God! Thank you so much!"

"I think she wanted to eat you alive," Brittany laughs, letting me go.

"I don't think I've ever felt so uncomfortable. I'm flattered but that was very unexpected and the way she looked at me, I wanted to jump your brother," I say, looking to him with a grin.

"I wouldn't have stopped you," he smiles and then grazes my arm with his.

"Gross!" Brittany says fake gagging. "I don't want that visual."

The waitress returns with our drinks and quickly walks away. It's beginning to get quite crowded now. "I thought we were going to eat before drinking," I nod at the shots. Brittany smiles and shrugs. "I'll be right back. I need to eat. Anyone want anything?" Brittany shakes her head and throws back her shot. "I'll come with you," Nick says. We walk towards the bar area where you place food orders. There are about ten people ahead of us.

"So, Brittany says you know the drummer," I say, trying to make conversation.

"Yeah. I went to college with Drew. He's a good guy and very smart. We studied a lot together.

"Is that code for partied?"

Nick laughs, "No, well sometimes but we had some hard classes together and had to keep up."

"I'm hoping to start some online classes in business soon."

"That's cool," he says smiling. "Why haven't I met you before?"

"I saw Brittany last week at the bank. We hadn't seen each other in a few years." I didn't want to go into the long story of dropping out and being consumed with Tyler. Not a great topic. We finally make it to the bar and I order a chicken sandwich and some fries. I look to Nick, "Are you having anything?"

"No, I just thought I'd come with you in case the waitress tried to take you to the back or something," he smiles.

"Well, that was nice of you." I return the smile.

After eating, and a few more shots, I feel great, very tipsy.

"Wanna dance?" Nicks asks me.

I think about it and decide what the hell. What would the harm be? He seems nice and he's hot. It should be fun. "Sure." He takes my hand and we head for the dance floor. The band is pretty awesome. They are a bit rock and pop together. The song playing is fast and has a lot of bass. I love it. Nick wraps one arm around my waist and pulls me closer to him. We are having a great time. He smiles at me and I smile back. He twirls me and now my back I pressed against his front. He's grinding on me and I think I feel how excited he is to be dancing with me. I drop down and pop back up and turn facing him again. He has a shocked look on his face.

"What?" I ask.

"Nothing," he smiles. "I didn't know you could dance like that."

"Well, you really don't know me," I laugh.

The song changes and it's even more energizing. We continue dancing and I look in the crowd and see Brittany, only she's not alone. Alex is beside her and he doesn't look happy. The song ends and we make our way back to Brittany, and now Alex. I've worked up a thirst.

"Hey Alex," Nick says. "I didn't know you were coming." Alex looks at me and then at Nick. "I thought I'd stop in and see what all the fuss was about. Hi, Jessa," he looks at me.

"Hi," I smile.

"Y'all were quite the dance team out there," he says, nodding toward the dance floor. He has a bit of a tone when saying it. Is he jealous?

"Do you dance?" I ask.

He hesitates, "I do."

"Well, let's see what you've got then," I smile challenging him.

He grins. "I don't want to put Nick to shame," he counters, looking at Nick.

Nick dies laughing. "I think I'll have to see this."

Well that's two of us. I want to see what his body can do.

"Are you chicken?" I start flapping my arms. He shakes his head smiling, grabbing my arm and leading me to the floor. We are further apart than I'd like. He can dance. I move a step closer and he grins, also moving closer to me. I can now smell the scent of his cologne. I take a deep breath and savor his scent. He moves a little closer and wraps his arms around my waist. We're now so close and he's grinding into me and I'm so turned on. One of his legs goes between mine to get us even closer. I can feel the heat of his leg on my pussy and it's making me wet. I wrap my arms around him and smell his neck and a small moan escapes. He grips my hips and pulls me onto him. I'm now grinding on his leg. I'm so turned on right now. I can't believe we're doing this. I will have to face him tomorrow sober and it makes me wonder how much he's had to drink tonight. I'm not going to think about it. I'm enjoying this night so much. He looks down into my eyes and I swallow hard. He leans forward and presses his lips to my ear. "You look beautiful tonight." It causes me to shiver. My panties are drenched. All he has to do is put pressure on my clit and I'll explode. One of his hands slides down to my ass and he squeezes. I let out a sigh.

"Do you like that, Jessa? Are you turned on?" I feel like I'm in a daze or trance so I nod speechless. He lifts my chin to meet his gaze and his eyes move down to my lips. "I want to kiss you Jessa. I've wanted to kiss you since you answered your door almost naked."

We're no longer dancing, but standing in the middle of the floor with strobe lights flashing around us. I'm staring into his eyes unable to blink, waiting for him to make a move only he doesn't.

"What's wrong?" I ask, disappointed. I want this. I want

him to kiss me.

"Jessa, there's a lot you don't know about me. I've had a rough few years and I can't jump into this with you. I do feel something for you and it scares me. Can I talk with you about it when I'm ready? I haven't talked to anyone about it other than my family." He looks pained and all I can do is nod. He gives me a small smile and kisses my cheek, taking my hand in his walking us back to the bar.

Brittany is right where we left her. Nick is now gone. I spot him not too far away talking to some slutty looking girl who hardly any clothes on. We all have switched to water and enjoy the rest of the show. I catch Alex looking at me a few times and I smile back at him. I look at his lips disappointed he didn't kiss me on the dance floor. It would have been perfect. He must know how wet he got me. I push the thought out of my head and enjoy the show, because otherwise, they will, torture me.

CHAPTER SIX

I'm up at the crack of dawn, way before I should be. I had a hard time sleeping after Alex teased me so much last night. I had some time with Bob and it didn't help much. I'm more nervous today about seeing him again, than I was Monday. I don't know what to expect when I get there or how he will act towards me.

I ring the doorbell and he answers with a cup of coffee in his hand and a small smile across his face.

"Good morning, Jessa." He hands me the cup in his hand.

"Good morning. Thank you," I smile, walking inside. I smell bacon. It's heavenly.

"I thought you might have breakfast with me before you start this morning."

"Sure. That's so sweet of you," I say following him into the kitchen. He pulls out my chair for me and I sit. I'm not used to this at all. He's such a gentleman.

"I had a really nice time with you last night and I regret not kissing you," Alex says, looking at my lips. "I couldn't fall asleep because I was thinking of you." He looks down at his plate, maybe a bit embarrassed.

"I didn't, either, actually. You kind of left me hanging, ya know?" I grin trying to make him more comfortable. He wasn't this shy last night.

"There's a lot I need to tell you before we even pursue this but I need time. I am a very private man and it's hard to talk about. I hope you can understand and give me time?"

He's waiting for my reply and I can't help but wonder what he needs to tell me.

"I understand. There's a lot we don't know about each other. There's no need to rush into anything. I had a pretty hard break up recently and I'm not trying to jump into another relationship."

"Okay. I'm glad to hear you say that," he sighs. "I really like you, Jessa. I haven't been in a relationship in quite a while and I'm just nervous." I can't help but smile. He's so adorable when he's nervous.

We finish our breakfast in silence, glancing at each other a few times. I stand with my plate and walk around to him, picking up his and putting them in the sink. When I turn around he's watching me. I can tell he's thinking. He looks down my body and stands, walking towards me.

"I know I said I wanted to take it slow, but I can't get the thought of kissing you out of my head."

He lifts my chin and looks deep into my eyes as if he's searching for my permission. I take a deep breath and move forward a couple of inches. He meets me half way and his lips touch mine. He pushes forward kissing me so passionately I feel myself melting into him. He wraps his arm around me and pulls me closer. I moan, feeling his hardness pressed against my stomach. I grab his shirt and pull him closer and his tongue slides into my mouth. He wraps his other arm around me and lifts me onto the counter, not breaking the kiss. My hands go into his hair and I pull slightly as he moans into my mouth. I know this is too soon and we need to slow down, but I want him so badly right now. I'd let him fuck me right here right now if he'd allow it. He pulls away a bit, breaking the kiss, both of us panting. He runs his hand down the side of my face gently and I press into his hand, looking into his eyes. He smiles at me. "I knew that was gonna be amazing," he says, giving me one last peck.

"Um, yeah, I think that's an understatement," I giggle. He helps me down from the counter and I regain the feeling in my legs. That was the best kiss I'd ever had in my life. It felt like fireworks going off all around us. I already want more of him.

"I'm sorry. I shouldn't have allowed it to go that far," he says, immediately looking away.

I furrow my brow not sure why he'd said that. Did he not feel what I felt? I think there could be something between us. I want to pursue this. I hope he feels the same way. He can't kiss me like that and then become so distant. It's like he shut his feelings off. I can't deal with this right now. I grab my cleaning supplies and go up the stairs not looking back.

I am beyond pissed right now, and when I'm pissed I can get some shit done. I'm in the master bedroom, making the bed, when I hear Alex come in.

"Jessa, I didn't mean to upset you. I'm just scared. You may never want to see me again, once I tell you everything."

"Okay, so when do you think you'll tell me? Because this is gonna piss me off quickly. I just gave in to my feelings and you shut me down. That hurts and I've dealt with enough of that recently." I'm angry and I can't help it. I'm embarrassed at how he just turned his back on me in the kitchen.

He's watching me and seems to want to say something but instead stalks over to me and grabs me quickly around the waist and pushes me back onto his bed. He's lying on top of me staring into my eyes. He caught me off guard. I'm speechless and just stare at him waiting to see what he's going to do.

"Do you know how incredibly sexy and adorable you are when you're pissed?"

I search his face. I don't like being told I'm adorable when I'm mad. It pisses me off more. I won't be mad though because he's right where I want him to be.

"Jessa, I know I need to take it slow with you but when I'm with you that all goes out the window. I just want to forget about all of that and be with you."

"Then just do it. Forget for now and just be with me."

"Would it be okay to kiss you again? I can't get over our first kiss. I want more."

"You don't have to ask to kiss me, just do it," I giggle.

"I don't want to do anything you don't want me too," he says looking me over but landing on my mouth.

"I want it all," I say, releasing the breath I didn't know I was holding.

"You don't know what you're saying Jessa." He looks pained.

"I said, quit thinking and just do." I raise up on my elbows to show him I want this. I don't understand this man. He's so confusing. I lean into him and he finally kisses me again. My hands instantly grab ahold of his hair, deepening the kiss. Our tongues mingle together and his hands move down to my jeans, unbuttoning them then slowly pulling them down my legs. He grabs my ass in both hands and squeezes. I moan and arch into his body. I'm so turned on. He's definitely an ass man. I've never had a guy pay so much attention to my backside before. He's kneading it in his hands. Each time, his fingers get closer to an area that's never been explored by a man before. Tyler thought anal was disgusting. The feeling is different, but good different. I think I'd let him do whatever he wanted to me at this moment. I'm so impatient and longing for his touch. We continue the kiss of a lifetime and he pulls away, lifting my shirt over my head.

"May I?" He's looking at my boobs.

"Yes. Please stop asking me. It's cute but not right now." I'm breathless and want whatever he's planning; though. I get the feeling he doesn't have a plan. He reaches behind me and I arch further so he can remove my bra. He unclasps it and my boobs are freed.

"So beautiful," he says before putting his mouth around one and circling the nipple with his tongue. He moves to the other, giving equal attention. It feels so good. He nibbles and I gasp at the feeling. It hurts a bit at first, but quickly changes to a good feeling. I move so he can do the same thing to my other nipple. He does and I moan, arching further into his mouth. I reach down towards his jeans and can feel his length across my hand. I rub across him and he moans and presses himself further into hand. I try to unzip his pants and he grabs, my stopping me.

"I want this to be about you. I've been imagining this for a while. Please just let me."

He continues his licking and sucking as he moves his way down my stomach, nipping as he goes. It tickles and I'm a squirming mess. He gets onto his knees, looking up at me. He looks like a predator and I'm his prey. Funny, because I think he's about to eat me alive and I can't wait. I've never had oral before. I don't know what's wrong with the couple of guys I'd been with. None of them would ever do it but I was also too embarrassed to ask them to, or ask why they wouldn't.

"Spread your legs for me," he whispers. I do as he says

and feel a bit on display. It makes me self-conscious and I'm so nervous. I thank God I wore a cute bra and matching panty set today. He spreads me open with his fingers. He looks up at me. "So ready for me." He licks his lips and I think I might cum right now seeing him there licking his lips. He's so hot and he wants me. Me! His head disappears and his mouth clamps down over my clit and sucks lightly. I scream and start to squirm. He stops what he's doing and looks up with concern. "Are you okay?"

Breathlessly I say, "Yes, I'm fine. Please don't stop."

I'm extremely sensitive to this feeling. Bob has nothing on Alex's tongue. I may be ruined. He continues his torture. He licks me and sucks and nibbles on my lips. That sends me overboard. I cry out so loudly I can't believe it's coming from me. I've never been so responsive to a man during sex. This is only Alex's tongue. I can't imagine what it will feel like when he's inside me. Alex laps up my juices as I come down from the best orgasm I've ever had.

Alex crawls up the bed and lays beside me looking at me. I'm trying to catch my breath and still have a lightheaded feeling. I turn to him and kiss him not even thinking of where his mouth just was. I taste myself on his lips. It's a very different taste. I don't exactly like it but don't mind kissing him like this. "That was amazing," I manage to say between breaths.

"I'm glad you enjoyed it. You taste delicious," he smiles licking his lips and my eyes go right to his mouth.

"That's the first time that anyone's ever..." I pause, embarrassed.

"What! Are you serious?"

"Yes, none of the guys I'd been with ever did it." I look down embarrassed I told him that fact.

"That's a damn shame, Jessa. You taste delicious. Best I've ever tasted." He kisses me again before saying, "You may be my new addiction."

"I think that would be fine with me," I giggle. "That was the best orgasm I've ever had."

"That won't be the last, I promise."

"I should get back to work ya know."

"I only hired you twice a week so I could see you more," he smiles and then laughs.

"I wondered why you had me coming twice. I figured it was for the laundry and that you were OCD," I laugh. He rolls on top of me and starts tickling me.

"I'm not that OCD. I can make you cum twice, though. I still have one to go," he laughs.

I'm screaming and flopping around underneath him from the torture. "No. no. I can't handle anymore right now. I'm too sensitive." I can still feel my clit throbbing. "Seriously though, I can't do that. I'm fine with spending time with you. I'd really enjoy it actually but I can't be paid that much for not working."

"Okay. How about you do what you do on Monday's and then I pay you by the hour on Thursday's and after you finish working we can just spend time together?"

"That works for me," I say, getting up looking for my panties. I don't see them.

"Looking for something?" He has a mischievous look on his face.

"Where's my panties?"

"I'm not sure," he smiles.

"What did you do with them?" I'm a bit annoyed now.

"I think I may keep them. Seeing you working and knowing you're not wearing them will be fun for me."

I scrunch my face up. "Will I get them back before the day is over or are you one of those creepy guys with a drawer full of women's panties."

"Jessa, you are the only woman I've had any relationship with in almost three years. I don't have a drawer full of panties, either. You can look if you'd like," he says, nodding towards his dresser.

I decide to do just that. I open the first two drawers and I see socks and boxers neatly folded. "Not OCD, huh?" I raise a brow. He hops off the bed stopping me from opening the next drawer. "Something to hide?"

"Jessa, I need to tell you something." He's suddenly very serious.

"Is this where the panties are?" I giggle.

"Yes." He looks at the floor.

"What! Are you kidding right now?"

He grabs my shoulders looking into my eyes. "I don't

want to talk too much about it right now, but I was married for four years and she suddenly passed away. I haven't removed any of her clothes from the drawers yet. It's been hard for me to let go, hard for me to talk about or really move forward."

"I'm so sorry, Alex. I completely understand. I would never push you. Please know that."

"Thank you. I've been alone for a long time now and it's just been difficult to deal with everything."

"When you're ready to tell me I'll listen." I kiss his cheek walking away.

"I'm going to go put the clothes in the dryer okay? Commando," I smile.

He gives me the biggest smile I've seen yet. I'll give him the time he needs. I couldn't imagine losing the person I love and then trying to move on with someone else. I do think it's a bit weird that I haven't seen any pictures of her while cleaning. Maybe it's hard for him to have the reminders around.

Soon after our time upstairs I find him in his office working on his laptop. I walk in with my dust spray and a rag. He looks up and smiles and I smile back. I grab a chair in the corner to start dusting the shelves behind him. I hear his chair swivel. I glance behind me quickly to see him staring at my ass. I reach up high to extend my body pushing my ass out a bit to give him a little show.

"Ya know, I may order you one of those sexy little

outfits to wear while you're here."

I start laughing and turn around facing him almost losing my balance and gasping as he jumps up to catch me.

"You can't distract me when I'm working," I giggle.

"I could say the same thing," he replies, arching a brow at me and squeezing my ass.

His lips crush against mine and I wrap my arms around him. Standing in this chair we're the same height. He's much taller than me. My breathing quickens and I feel my body begin to react to his kisses. He is such a good kisser. His tongue is larger than mine and as they twist together. I grow wet, remembering how good he was at licking my pussy. I let go of his shoulders and step off the chair. I want to please him like he had me. I'm not sure if he will let me but I'm going to try. He couldn't possibly deny me. I look up into his eyes and stand on my tip toes for one more kiss before dropping to my knees. I peer up at him and the look on his face is surprise and maybe desire. I unzip his jeans and slowly lower them, dropping them to the floor.

"Jessa, you don't have to do this."

"I know that. I want to." I want to see him and feel him in my mouth.

I drag his boxers down his legs and his dick springs free almost hitting me in the face. I wasn't expecting that. He's not massively huge, but he's much bigger than the others I've seen. I'm contemplating how I'll be able to fit all of him in my mouth. I hold him in one hand and cup his balls in the other, lightly squeezing and he sighs. I look up at him as I flick my tongue across the small drop of cum glistening on the head and he moans. I bring the head just inside of my mouth and he moans as I squeeze his balls again. His breathing picks up and I can tell he's trying to hold back a bit. I'm not having that. I move forward taking him all the way to the back of my throat, my nose hitting his abs. I suck hard and he moans again, louder this time. I drag him out only to go again more quickly, but not all the way, and I swallow. He moans and bucks forward almost choking me. His hands fist in my hair and I allow him to take my mouth as he pleases.

"I'm close, Jessa" he pants. He tries to pull out and I grab both ass cheeks holding him in place. I've never wanted to swallow before. I'm curious about the taste. I've heard it tastes disgusting but for Alex I don't care. I want it too. I begin a slow torture of sucking hard and deep and I feel his legs shaking, his moans are more urgent. I flick the head once more and go deep and I feel the warm liquid hitting the back of my throat and I swallow quickly. I go down once more and suck him dry, looking up at him. His face is so sexy right now. I could almost cum with the pure satisfaction I've given him. He lifts me to my feet and holds me in his arms kissing me so fiercely as he tries to catch his breath.

"That was amazing Jessa. You did something with your tongue and wow, that was awesome." I start giggling and kiss his mouth once more.

"I'm glad you enjoyed it," I smile shyly. I don't like being complimented about oral, but with him I do. It feels good to know I'd pleased him as much as he had me.

I swat him on the shoulder smiling. "Now, let me get back to work."

"Yes ma'am," he salutes me, sitting back down at his desk. I can hear him still trying to get his breathing under control. It makes me happy to know I'd affected him so much.

I finish for the day and walk back into his office. He's facing the window away from me. I don't mean to eavesdrop but I wanted to let him know I'm finished and need to be paid for the day.

"I'm scared to tell her, Brittany. What if she hates me?" he pauses. Brittany is speaking now. "I really like her. I don't want to hurt her." I wish I knew what she was saying. I decide to leave. I don't want to stand here and have him turn around and know I'd heard their conversation. I walk to the kitchen and sit at the table. I hope he finishes quickly. I want to get home to see if the test results have been posted. I forgot the ID number or I'd do it now on my phone.

A few minutes later he walks in the kitchen smiling at me. "Are you finished?"

"Yes. Will I get my panties back now?" I scowl him.

"Can I keep them as a souvenir?"

"Seriously? I guess," I laugh.

"Would you like to stay for dinner? I could order in?"

"I'd love to, but I need to get home to check my grades from the tests I took the other day.

"Oh okay." He sounds a bit disappointed. "What tests did you take?" Fuck I didn't want him to know. "I took my GED the other day and I'm hoping the results are posted." I fidget not looking at him. I don't want him to know I didn't graduate.

He walks over to me. "Hey, look at me." He grabs my chin and says, "Don't be ashamed Jessa. I'm sure you did great," he smiles.

"Thanks. I hope I did. I want to take some classes and start in business."

"That's great, Jessa. I'm proud of you."

I smile. I guess it was stupid to be embarrassed to tell him. He doesn't seem to think less of me.

"Let me know how you did and we can all go out and celebrate."

"Okay. I will. That sounds nice. I'll see you soon," I say, kissing him and walking to my car.

What a day this has been. I had fantasies of how this day would be, but I never expected any of them to actually happen. I got my first orgasm from oral. I finally saw his dick and I even swallowed. It wasn't as bad as I thought it would be. I laugh at the thought.

I make it home and rush to my mom's office and log in. Damn it! They're not up yet. I guess it will be tomorrow. I should've just stayed with Alex. There's no telling what we could be doing right now. I text him to let him know.

Hey! The results aren't posted yet.

See you should've stayed for dinner.

Lol! I should have. What would we have eaten?

Well I would've had you.

Maybe tomorrow ;)

I hope so. Have a good night.

You too!

CHAPTER SEVEN

I walk into the office first thing after waking up. Yes! The scores are up. I fucking passed! I am so excited. I knew I did well, but having the validation just makes it better. I call my mom first and it goes to voicemail. She's probably in court and can't answer. I decide to text Brittany and tell her, too.

Hey! I passed my GED. I just got the results in.

That's awesome! We need to celebrate tonight :)

Sounds great to me. Let me know later and we can decide.

Ok. I will.

I think about texting Alex next. He said for me to let him know. I guess I could send him a text too. That wouldn't be weird.

Hi! I passed!

I'm proud of you.

Brittany wants to get together later. Want to join us?

Sure. How about I take you to dinner? I know a great place.

Ok. That sounds nice :)

Great! I'll make reservations and pick you up at 7:00. I'll let Brittany know too.

Ok. Sounds fun. Thank you!

It will be :)

There's something so adorable when a man uses a smiley in texts. I'm excited to have plans with them tonight. I have no idea where he's taking me but I need to find something to wear. If he's making reservations then we're not eating at the café. I have plenty of time and need to consider the business classes I want to enroll in.

—

I find a cute skirt and top to wear for tonight. I straighten my hair and put on a little makeup. I grab a leather jacket that matches the boots I've chosen, and walk down stairs. I sit on the bench in the entry way to swap out my purses and put my boots on. I see Alex pull up and smile. I wonder what this night will bring. I hope more kisses and maybe even more. He rings the doorbell and I hobble over with one boot on. He smiles and looks me over. "You look amazing," he says, then points at my feet smiling. "You're missing a boot." I laugh at him and raise it in the air. I sit back down and put the boot on zipping up the side and look up at him and he's watching me.

He walks over to me. "Those are the sexiest boots I think I've ever seen. Is your mom here?"

"No. She basically lives with her boyfriend." I see relief wash over his face.

He bends down and kisses me softly. "We'd better go. We have a seven thirty reservation."

"Where are we going?"

"A great steakhouse in town." He sees my face falter. "They have other stuff. too."

He doesn't get that's not why I'm concerned. There's only one steakhouse that does reservations, and I would like to avoid it.

We pull up and it's that steakhouse. I wonder if I can say I'm not feeling well and go back home. I don't want to be here. I know Tyler works on Friday nights. Maybe he doesn't work here anymore.

We are greeted and seated immediately by the hostess. Alex pulls out my chair for me and I smile and take a seat. “Such the gentlemen.” He returns the smile and sits next to me, pouring us each a glass of wine I’ve never heard of, or could even pronounce. He’s thought of everything tonight. Brittany hasn’t arrived yet.

“Have you talked to Brittany?” I ask, looking around the room for Tyler.

“She said she’d be a few minutes late. Are you okay?”

“My ex works here.”

“Do you want to go somewhere else? I can call Brittany and let her know. We could even go back to my place,” he teases trying to help my mood.

I laugh. “I’ll be fine.”

“Well y’all look like you need to get a room,” Brittany says, walking up and my mouth drops open.

“I told her we could go back to my house.”

“Gross! I don’t need to hear this when I’m about to eat,” she fake gags.

I start laughing, The server returns and says, “Your waiter will be right with you,” smiling at Alex before walking away. I sigh, hoping it won’t be Tyler.

A few minutes later, I smell his cheap cologne before I see him. He comes up behind me and Brittany’s eyes bulge, immediately looking at me. I shake my head slightly.

“Well, well.,well. You haven’t changed much,” Brittany

frowns.

"Thanks! Neither have you," Tyler says, thinking she was flirting with him.

"It wasn't a compliment," she says rudely, looking over her menu.

Everyone's ordered but me. Alex looks at me and gives me a small smile.

"Ma'am, do you know what you would like," he walks closer to me, to see my face. His eyes bulge and he looks to Brittany and then Alex probably sizing him up.

"I'll have the chicken parmesan." I don't look at him, instead I smile at Alex. Tyler walks away and I let out the breath I didn't realize I was holding.

"Jessa, I don't get what you ever saw in that douche." I start laughing and so does she. Alex just looks at us with a weird look on his face. I'm not sure what he's thinking at the moment. We go quiet as Tyler comes back with our salads.

"Do you need anything else?"

"No," Brittany bites back and Tyler leaves the table. I bet he knows he isn't getting a tip from our table tonight. I swear Brittany and I are so much alike.

"He's not getting a damn penny for a tip," she laughs. I shake my head giggling. I swear, Brittany and I are so much alike.

We enjoy our wine and salads and have small talk for a bit. Brittany finally opens her mouth about how friendly Alex and I are together. "So, what's up with y'all?"

"Well, Ms. Nosy, if you must know I really like your friend Jessa," he says, blushing and looks at Brittany. She is looking at him with an unspoken question. Alex shakes his head and she frowns and then looks at me and smiles. "Well, she is pretty great, if I get a say." As she says it her plate was set in front of her. I look up and see Tyler with a pissed look on his face. As he places my plate down he asks, "Can I uh, talk to you for a minute please?"

"No. I'm about to eat." I look at him like he's stupid. He then looks at Alex and sets his plate down. "Let me know if you need anything else," he says before walking away.

We enjoy our meals and Tyler sets the check down and hurries away. Alex quickly grabs if and inserts his credit card. Tyler comes back a few minutes later for the check, looking at me as he walks away. We finish the bottle of wine and again Tyler sets the check back down and walks away.

"You aren't actually leaving him a tip, are you?" Brittany asks.

Alex looks up at her, "I am, actually. Do you want to know what it is?" He's smiling now.

"I told him thanks for fucking up because now I can have a chance with Jessa," he states, looking at me. I smile shyly.

"Awwww. Isn't that fucking adorable," Brittany giggles and gags. "So when did this happen? Wait don't answer that. I had a feeling y'all were gonna hit it off. You're welcome." She takes a bow as we walk out to the parking lot.

"Well, I'll see y'all later. Don't have too much fun without me." She abruptly pauses, then frowns. "That didn't sound right at all," she says, shaking her head; we all laugh. I look at Alex and then to the pavement. I have no idea what we are going to do now. I didn't think past dinner.

Brittany leaves but not before blowing her horn and laughing as she speeds away.

Alex opens my door and I climb inside. I think I need a step ladder it's so tall. He gets in and puts the keys in the ignition, but before starting the truck he turns to me. "What do you want to do now?" He seems nervous and I find it adorable.

"I don't know, what do you want to do?

"We could go get ice cream or something?" "How about or something," I smile, leaving it to whatever he thinks I mean.

He looks at me maybe a little shocked but he smiles. I think he's contemplating what to say next. I see it all over his face.

"I know I've said it before, but I really like you, Jessa, and I like spending time with you. I haven't had such strong feelings for a woman in quite a while and I'm not sure what to do about it. I know I told you my wife died, but I didn't want to tell you the whole story and I feel that I need to tell you some of that, before anything else happens between us. Okay?"

I nod, waiting for him to start. I just don't know what

could make him so sure I'd not want to be with him, but I'm about to find out.

"Lizzy was my wife's name. We grew up together and after college we started dating. Shortly after, she took a job up north and we did the long-distance relationship thing and it wasn't easy for us. She cheated and when I found out I was devastated. To get my revenge I started cheating." He pauses and looks out the window away from me. "She was gone for about five years and then moved back, we had stayed together despite everything that happened. I'm not sure why, exactly. We seemed to have grown apart some, and I wanted us to be like we were before she moved away, so I proposed, thinking it would solve all our problems. We moved in together and it was hard. We were polar opposites in every way and I mean in every way possible. We were married for a total of nine months when we finally separated. I was happier and so was she. She called one day, wanting to meet and talk about us. I assumed she was serving me with divorce papers. Her car was in the shop so I picked her up and we went to have dinner and try to keep it civil. She drops a bomb on me telling me she was actually pregnant. I was floored, but we decided to try and make it work. I even agreed to counseling." I see tears begin to form in his beautiful eyes and I want to hold him close. I grab his hand instead to show him I'm here for him.

"We were on our way home when a deer jumped out onto the road and I swerved and hit a tree. We were both injured badly, but Lizzy had hit her head on the windshield and had bleeding on her brain. The swelling was so severe that the doctors couldn't perform surgery. She died two days later."

I honestly have no idea what to say, but I try, "Alex I'm so sorry about your wife and child. That's a terrible tragedy." I can't imagine how hard that must have been for him. I can see the pain in his eyes. Death is a horrible thing to go through.

"Jessa, there's more, but can we please talk about it some other time and enjoy or time together?"

"Yes, of course," I say, scooting closer to him. I wipe the straggling tear away and caress his cheek. His eyes close and I kiss his forehead. We stay like this for a few minutes.

He eventually looks up at me, "I am so thankful to have you." I smile and he kisses me tenderly. As he pulls away I nibble and suck on his bottom lip. He instantly looks up at me and his eyes darken. "Do you want to come over for a while, maybe have a drink?"

I act like I'm thinking it over, even though I already know my answer. "Yes. I'd love too."

"I didn't tell you how beautiful you look tonight. You are stunning," he says, taking my hand in his and bringing it to his lips.

Alex drives out of the parking lot, heading for his house. It's not far from the restaurant. His hand still in mine, I rest them in my lap. I suddenly have an idea. I slowly take his hand and drag it over the inside of my thigh, rising my skirt as I do so. He looks at me quickly and then back at the road. I spread my legs further and move my panties to one side. I see him glance down to see what I'm doing before focusing back on the road. I adjust so his hand barely hovering, so close that I can feel the warmth of it on me. I drag his hand down my wetness and look over at him.

"Fuck, Jessa. You're so wet." He doesn't look at me, instead, focusing on the road. I push one finger inside and moan. He then takes control and my torture is over. He moves his finger inside and his palm is putting pressure on my clit. He adds another finger and increases speed, rubbing my clit with his thumb. Suddenly, he curves his fingers upward and wiggles them quickly. It feels fucking amazing, and with his thumb still on my clit, I lose control and burst into pleasure around his fingers, moaning loudly.

Shortly after, I'm awakened to Alex lifting me in his arms. I must have dozed off. That's never happened before. "It's alright, Jessa. I've got you." I relax in his arms and lay my head on his shoulder. His cologne is heavenly. He carries me upstairs to his bedroom and lays me on the bed. I watch him remove his button-up shirt and now he's got my attention. I watch him strip in front of me, making a pile on the floor. I smile sleepily at him and raise up on my elbows. I feel like I should pinch myself to wake up from a dream. He just can't be real. Looking down his gorgeous body I feel myself getting wet again. I want him. He sees me admiring him and flexes and then throws out a chuckle. He's messing with me. It's the sexiest cutest fucking thing ever. I feel my face heat because he caught me and I look away. I don't know why I'm embarrassed. I shouldn't be.

"So, where's the drink I came for?" I joke waiting for his response. He gives me a weird look and I laugh. "I'm just joking."

He saunters over to the bed with his eyes on me, examining me. The look in his eyes, I think he wants to devour me.

"Jessa, I need to tell you something," he says, sitting beside me on the bed.

"One of the many reasons Lizzy and I didn't work out had a lot to do with my sexual needs," he clears his throat. He's nervous. "I tend to be a little rough." He says it so softly; I almost didn't hear him. I've never had it rough. I've wanted it that way, but Tyler seemed to do the exact opposite. Our sex life really sucked. I don't know what to say.

"Are you open to that, Jessa? Will you give it a try, give me a chance?"

He holds my face in his hands gazing into my eyes and kisses me deeply melting my panties. He pulls away, looking over my face and waiting for my reply.

"Yes." That's all I have a chance to say before he's on top of me, smiling down at me. I feel his erection pushing into my stomach. I grab his ass cheeks and squeeze hard, my nails digging into him. He hisses before kissing me again.

Our tongues tangle and he pulls my hair to one side and kisses down my neck, then nibbles his way across my collar bone. His hand goes under my shirt lightly tickling his way up to my breasts, leaving goosebumps along the way. He squeezes one and reaches for the other. They aren't too big so his large hand is able to caress both. I arch into him, closing my eyes, enjoying how he makes my body feel. He stops and looks down at me with a devilish grin. I'm not scared. I know he wouldn't hurt me. I'm curious and excited.

He drags my panties down my legs, leaving just my skirt on, as he spreads me wide. I am so glad I shaved everywhere.

He grunts his approval. "I like it bare like this," he says before slapping my pussy causing a moan to leave my throat. He raises up and takes his jeans and boxers off quickly. He positions himself over me, holding his hard dick in his hand, rubbing it against my wetness. I want him so badly. I wrap my legs around his waist, pulling him to me. The look on his face is weird. Did I do something wrong? He winces.

"Jessa, I just remembered I don't have any condoms."

"It's really okay. I'm on the shot, so I don't think we should worry. I'm clean. I assume you are, also?"

"I am, but do you think that's a good idea?" His eyebrows are furrowed and he looks adorable.

"I'm so fine with it. I want to feel all of you."

He moans and buries himself inside of me, causing me to moan loudly. He's much bigger than Tyler. Ugh! Stop thinking about him Jessa!

"Fuck, Jessa, you're so wet," he moans. "Your pussy feels so good," he says, driving into me. I wrap my legs around him again and squeeze my walls around him tightly. I can already feel my orgasm building. Alex starts rubbing circles into my clit as I moan.

"Are you close, Jessa? You feel too good: too good. I'm not gonna last long."

"Yes. I'm close," I pant. He's pounding into me now. His pelvis brushing against my clit. It feels so fucking good like this. Suddenly, I feel my legs beginning to quiver. I squeeze him tighter and wrap my arms around his back. It hits me and I combust, screaming his name, digging my nails into his back and my heels into his ass. My orgasm milks him inside of me. He moans deeply and I feel his warm cum filling me. He collapses on top of me, his weight on his elbows so he doesn't smash me.

"Alex, that was fucking amazing!"

"It was. You feel so good."

We're both still trying to catch our breath but he gets up and goes into the bathroom returning with a warm wash cloth. He spreads my legs and cleans me up. It surprises me that he would think to do that for me. He tosses it into the hamper and returns to the bed lying beside me, looking at me.

"Are you okay? Was I too rough?"

"I'm fine, more than fine, actually. That was the best

I've ever had," I sigh.

"It was for me, too."

I snuggle into his side, we lay there quietly and doze off.

CHAPTER EIGHT

The morning sun is shining through Alex's bedroom window. I roll over to find that Alex is still sleeping. I can finally look at him and not feel embarrassed. I shouldn't anymore, after what we shared last night. He has the cutest nose. I skim my fingers across his face. He stirs a bit, but doesn't wake up. I can see his morning tent rising from the sheet causing me to giggle. He slowly opens one eye looking at me. "What's so funny?" His voice is deeper when he wakes up.

"Nothing, really. I was just watching you sleep," I say, looking down at the tent.

"Hhhhhmmmmmm. Is that so? I think someone's happy to see you this morning," he laughs.

"Um. I doubt that. I think you just need to go pee," I say, shaking my head swatting his ass.

He gets up and heads to the bathroom. I get up and grab my clothes from the floor getting dressed before he comes back out. He comes out and looks disappointed.

"What's wrong?"

"I thought we'd lay in bed for a while and cuddle." He

gives me a sad face. I start laughing at him. He runs over and swoops me up in his arms, kissing me, morning breath and all.

"I don't know how I can have such strong feelings for you, but I do and it still scares me. Is that weird?"

"I don't think so, because I also feel it. My last relationship was terrible and I'm scared too. I told myself months ago that that would be the last time I allowed myself to be so wrapped up in a man. I think I lied to myself," I smile.

"Jessa, I don't want to ever hurt you. I wouldn't ever cheat on you. I promise."

He looks so sincere, looking right into my eyes, I kiss his lips. "I hope not. I think it would ruin me."

He hugs me close, "Jessa would you be..." he pauses and takes a deep breath. "How do you feel about being mine?" I bite my bottom lip pondering the idea.

"I'd love to be yours," I answer, beaming at him. He kisses me quickly and most of it was my teeth causing me to giggle.

"Would you like some breakfast?"

"Sure. I'll need to go home and change first," I say, looking down at last night's outfit.

"Will your mom be there?"

"No. Why?" I don't know why he'd be asking me that.

"I just don't want to cause any problems," he sighs.

"How would you be causing problems?"

"Can we talk about it another time?" He sighs. "I'll make us breakfast."

"Okay. I guess. You're being kind of weird about my mom, though." He looks away. I don't know what to think. I don't want to overthink. My mind wanders.

"Please tell me you didn't date my mom or something?"

He laughs a little. "No. It's nothing like that. I promise. Can we just have a nice day? I don't want to think about the past. I want to enjoy my time with you today," he says, reaching for my hands. I look at him, trying to think what I should do. I don't want to be stupid this time around. I want nothing but honesty.

"Alex, I want to understand. I want to give you time. I just don't know how long I can wait. I don't want us to get serious and then you drop a bomb on me."

He looks at the floor. "I don't want that either."

We go down stairs and he makes us breakfast. I help clean up and then we sit out on the patio and talk, getting to know each other better. It's a beautiful sunny day today. We talk about our parents and school and stuff like that. His parents live up north a few hours away and he has a sister who's much older than him. He seems to have had a great childhood though.

I tell him about my dad leaving and how I screwed up by quitting school and wasting years on Tyler.

"How old are you Alex?"

"I'm almost twenty-nine."

"How do you own the construction company at such a young age?"

"Well, my dad built it first and a few years ago wanted more time with my mom so after a couple of years showing him I could handle the responsibility he passed ownership to me. That was two years ago."

"That's awesome."

"I hired Brittany shortly after to help me, and she does an amazing job. I don't go into the office much, which puts more work on her, but after Lizzy died and the way all that went down, I don't get out of the house too much. I was very depressed and people talked and it was just hard to show my face around town."

"I don't understand? I thought you said it was an accident?"

"It was, but there were many people who didn't believe that."

"Why?"

He sighs, and runs his hand through his hair. "That's the part I was trying to avoid talking about. I do need to tell you, so I might as well do it now."

"I won't judge you, Alex. That was in your past."

"Thank you." He holds my hands in his and takes a moment before starting. "What I didn't tell you was after the accident, Lizzy's parents accused me of purposely causing it to hurt Lizzy. They knew we were seperated for a while and didn't know about the dinner and that we were trying to work it out. They knew Lizzy was pregnant, though. I couldn't believe they had thought so low of me and that I would kill my wife and unborn child. It was a horrible slap in the face for me."

I squeezed his hand in support. "I'm so sorry."

"A couple of days after Lizzy died, her parents filed charges and I was arrested. Long story short, it went to trial but didn't take long to show that it was in fact an accident. The part that really makes this hard for us, though, is your mother was the attorney for Lizzy's parents."

My mouth falls open. "Oh my God! Now I get it. Do you think my mom would have a problem with you because of this?"

"Well, she was definitely trying to throw the book at me. Even though I was found not guilty, I think it bothered her she lost the case."

"Alex, if you were innocent I know she wouldn't have still thought you were guilty. She does hate losing cases, but because you were innocent it wasn't about that."

"Well, it's really none of her business. I'm a grown woman and can make my own decisions," I state flatly.

"That's true, but I don't want to come between you and your mom."

"You won't. She isn't a judgmental person. She will be fine, and if not she'll come around. I am not hiding you from her. So, this was the part you were so worried about?"

"It was. After I saw the pictures I was shocked. It's a

very small world."

"It is and in a small town in Arkansas, where everyone knows everyone she's bound to find out. I want to tell her, okay?"

"What if she hates me? She found out a lot about me, not all was bad, but she knows about my sexual preferences and knows that I had cheated on Lizzy. It didn't seem to matter that she had also cheated on me. It was all about making me look like a horrible person, and she definitely did that."

"She doesn't even know you. She has basically hearsay. She only knows the lies that people tried to pin on you. Don't worry." I move to sit on his lap in the deck chair.

"I'm so lucky to have you, Jessa," he says, kissing me. "Please just promise me you won't let her try to break us up. I care deeply for you."

"I promise I won't. I don't think she would do that, though. I already care so much for you and she can't change that." I want to say those three words because it's how I feel, but I think it's too soon. Our last relationships obviously weren't the best and I don't want to rush anything with him or become as wrapped up as I was before. It's not healthy. I need to continue to work on myself.

"I just worry when she sees me with you she's gonna flip out."

"Please stop being so paranoid. It will be fine."

"I hope you're right. So many people made me look like

a horrible person. I doubt she has any respect for me.

"Okay. How about I plan a dinner for us with my mom?" He doesn't reply. He just looks terrified, staring at me. "Alex, if we're gonna be together we're gonna have to do this."

"I know. I've just pretty much become a hermit after the case. People talked behind my back and the whispers and stares. It was just hard for me. That's the main reason I always work from home. I don't like the looks and I still get them sometimes. I just wish things were different and could just forget."

"I don't think it's healthy. You can't stay here 24-7."

"I don't. Sometimes I go to the pub or the bar."

"Oh yeah, those are places that can pass judgement with all the alcohol," I roll my eyes at him.

"We went to dinner though."

"Yeah and we were in the corner where hardly anyone could see us. I won't hide or stay here all the time, Alex. Who cares what people think, anyway?"

"My therapist said the same thing. It's not healthy and blah, blah, blah."

"What do they say now?"

He shrugs before looking away, "I stopped going."

"Why?"

"I didn't feel that it was helping me."

"I'm sure if you weren't making the effort it wouldn't have helped. You have to try. I'll help you. I'm going to help you," I smile. "I'm calling my mom and we're going to have dinner with her, if she doesn't have plans."

"Tonight?" He seems anxious.

"Yes, tonight. If you want to be with me you're going to try." I grab my phone off the table and call my mom's number. I put it on speaker looking at him as it rings.

On the third ring, she finally picks up, "Hi sweetie."

"Hi, mom. Do you have any plans for dinner?"

"No. We're just relaxing why?"

"Well, there's someone I want you to meet that means a lot to me."

"Oh. Okay. Have you met someone?"

"I have and he's wonderful," I say, looking up at Alex and seeing some of the tension leave his face.

"I'd love to. Where?"

"Can you meet us at the pub in town about seven?"

"Sure. I look forward to it. Love you."

"Love you, too, mom." I hang up.

We take a shower together and that is a first for me. I had never showered with Tyler. That was something else he thought was stupid. I think it was because he jacked off in the shower.

Alex washes my hair and my body. It is amazing to have someone want to do something like this for me. He pushes me up against the cold tiles and drops to his knees, kissing my stomach and making his way down to my now throbbing clit. Having him massaging my head and my body had gotten my blood flowing. I gripped his wet hair with one hand and his shoulder with the other for balance. The feeling of him devouring me, with the warm water trickling down my body is like nothing I've ever felt. I'm a panting mess. When my orgasm emerges, I'm shaking and my legs feel weak. He stands up and kisses me. I feel his dick against me and grab it firmly in my hand, causing him to moan in my mouth. I want to return the pleasure he'd just given me so I get down on my knees, just as he had just a few moments ago. Looking up at him, I bring him to my lips and lick the tip. The desire in his eyes is hypnotic.

I take him all the way to the back of my throat and swallow. I know he likes it when I do that.

"Oh fuck, Jessa," he says, gripping my head in his hands. He doesn't take control, even though I know he wants to. I can tell he's holding back. I repeat the movements and take his balls in my hand, massaging them as I begin to pick up my pace. He's panting and moaning and I feel his dick grow even harder. I know he's close so I suck even harder and faster. His legs begin to twitch a bit and I glance up at him. It's a beautiful sight. He has his head thrown back on the tiles and the water cascading down his body. I see the strain in his neck. He's so close now. I slow down and when he's almost about to slip out I flick my tongue across the head causing his legs to twitch each time I do it. He looks down at me and watches me torturing him. "I'm close, Jessa," he says between pants. I pick up the pace again and when a deep moan escapes. I pull him out and let him release all over my chest.

"That was so fucking hot, Jessa," he says, shaking his head as he helps me up. I stand under the water, watching him wash away. I'd always wanted to do that. I'm not sure why. I've read it in books a lot and know the guys always love it, so I thought I'd try it out. It was very erotic that's for sure. I want him inside me, but there's no time. We only have about thirty minutes until we meet my mom for dinner.

I think Alex is a bit more relaxed now but I can tell he's still nervous. He's asked me three different times if he looks okay and has changed just as many. I think it's cute he wants to impress her. I know he's concerned, but I think everything will be just fine.

CHAPTER NINE

We find a table and sit. I face the door so I can see when mom is walking in. I am a little nervous, now too. I don't want Alex to see it, though. I know she won't make a scene, with her reputation to protect. I wasn't stupid choosing a public place for her seeing him again.

The waitress walks up, "What can I get you to drink?" I think I need something strong. I made it sound okay introducing my mom to Alex, but now I'm not so sure.

"I'll have an apple Crown and cranberry, please." Alex looks at me quickly. I don't want him to know I'm nervous now, too.

"Make that two," Alex smiles and the waitress walks away to make our drinks. He glances over at me. "Are you okay?" he asks. I smile, to not seem as freaked as I am inside.

"I'm fine," I smile again. The waitress brings our drinks and I take a big gulp, not only because I'm nervous, but because it is my favorite drink. It's so yummy. I feel like I should've googled the case to be more prepared. I know Alex didn't lie to me. I just want to be prepared for what my mother is going to say. I should be ready. When it comes to me she's very protective. I am her only child.

"This is so good, Jessa," he says licking his lips. It makes me think of how good that tongue is on me.

"Isn't it! I love it. I was watching an author's live feed one night and he was drinking it so I thought I'd try it. I'm so glad I did. Makes me all warm inside," I grin.

"I am here," Mom says cheerfully, walking up. She can't see Alex yet, and I'm glad because his eyes now look like they could pop out of his head.

"Hi, mom," I say, getting up to hug her. "This is Alex," I say as she walks over to her seat.

The look on her face is utter shock and possibly fury. She quickly recovers, though.

"Well, this is a shock. Should I say it's nice to see you again?"

"Mom, please." She cuts me off quickly. "Is this the man you're dating?" she asks, looking at me. She's not happy at all.

"Yes, he is, mom. I know you already think you know him, but you only know what people wanted you to know."

"Oh no sweetie. I know quite a lot. There were quite a few witnesses that proved that. Do you even know what kind of man he is?" She's speaking as if he isn't sitting at this very table.

"Yes, I do," I say irritated. "I really like Alex and I hoped that you could get past all that and see he makes me happy."

She looks at Alex, "How did you meet my daughter?"

"Well, Ms. Phillips my niece gave me a number for someone to clean my house. I didn't know that it would be Jessa." He looks so uncomfortable right now. He did the throat clearing thing several times in that one sentence.

"Are you nervous, Alex?"

"Of course I am. I knew everything that happened during the case and what you think you know about me was going to make this very hard. I want you to know, that during the trial everyone made me out to be a monster. I am not who I was perceived to be. I care very much for your daughter." She looks at him for several seconds before speaking.

"So, you want to tell me that you didn't leave bruises on your wife during sex and that you weren't cheating on her?"

Alex looks down at the table. I want to say something to help him but I also want her to get past this. I know he can handle it, even though this is painful to see.

"I never cheated on Lizzy once we were married. We both cheated before, not that makes it okay, because it wasn't but you didn't know the whole story."

"What about the bruises? You kind of avoided that part," she says furiously.

"Lizzy and I had gotten a little rough one night and she bruised easily," he says flatly. I can tell he's getting embarrassed.

She narrows her eyes. "There were text messages between her and her friend as evidence in court, stating that you hurt her during whatever you do."

"If you'd known Lizzy at all you would know how much she exaggerates everything. We had different preferences in the bedroom. I don't know what you are expecting me to say here."

"Okay let me help you. Do you like to cause pain in your sexual favors?"

"No!" he says loudly. He looks around and notices people staring at us now. He leans forward towards my mom and says, "I would never hurt a woman, ever, and especially not the woman I'm falling in love with." He realizes what he's just said and looks at me. My mouth falls open. I don't know what to say. I want to say it back. I don't know if it's too soon. I'm scared and my mother is stunned looking between us. I wish it had happened at a different time, not here with my mother witnessing it.

"Jessa, I didn't mean for it come out here," he shakes his head and looks down at his fingers.

I look at my mom and back to Alex. "I feel the same way and didn't want to freak you out if you didn't feel it, too. I'm falling in love with you, too." I smile so big with tears in my eyes.

"Don't you think that's a little fast, Jessa? I mean how long have you even known him?"

And there it is. She's ruined our moment. I give her a go-to-hell look. "Mom, I don't need your input right now. You married dad very soon."

"Exactly my point. You see how that worked out."

"Mom, we're not getting married and even if we were, it's really none of your business."

"Wow. Jessa, what is the matter with you," she asks, shocked at my comment.

"I wanted you to have dinner with us and maybe try to get to know Alex for who he really is, not who everyone made him out to be. I'm not stupid. If I thought he'd hurt me in any way, we wouldn't be sitting here. Now, can you please let go of what you think you know and let us all start over like adults?"

Her face changes to one of regret. "I know you're a smart girl, Jessa. No, I don't know everything about Alex and if you feel this strongly, I'm willing to try." Looking to Alex she says, "I'm sorry for what I said, but you can't blame me. She's my daughter and I want what's best for her. If you can be the man she deserves in every way, then I'm okay with it, even though I don't think what I say would matter either way. If you do hurt her, though, I'll castrate you," she smiles and Alex's eyes bug out again. I laugh.

"Okay. So now that that's over, let's enjoy the night together. Mom, you'll be happy to know I'm enrolling in some business courses at the tech school in town on Monday. I should start soon," I smile. I know that will make her happy.

"That's wonderful honey! I'm proud of you."

"Ms. Phillips, I have my business degree and will help

her if she needs it. I doubt she will, though." That makes her eyebrows raise.

"See, mom, I told you, you didn't know everything about him. He is very smart and runs his father's business."

"Well, technically, it's my business now. My father retired and gave it to me. I work very hard to keep it running as he did."

"So, the house I dropped you off at your first day is Alex's house?" I can tell she's trying to piece it all together.

"Yes, it is. I built it shortly before Lizzy passed," he says sadly.

The waitress comes finally, to take our orders. They're quite busy tonight. We decide on one of the pizzas they're known for. They are huge and taste delicious.

"So, Alex, what's the plan with Jessa?"

"Mom! Really," I shake my head.

"I wasn't looking for anyone, Ms. Phillips. After Lizzy's passing I kept to myself. That case hurt my reputation around town, not that I care really. When Jessa came that first night to look at my house, I was shocked. As you know, she looks similar to Lizzy and that was kind of hard for me at first. When we shook hands that night, I felt something there and it scared me. She's slowly been helping me through a lot of things, and, that she probably doesn't even realize," he says, grabbing my hand and smiling at me. I am falling hard for him. I know it's fast, but I can't help what my heart feels.

The waitress brings our pizza and some waters for us. We eat our meal and talk about things that are much lighter and enjoyable like the crazy weather and the classes I'll soon be taking. Mom, shortly into conversation, drops a bomb on me, though.

"Jessa, I do have some news I don't think you'll be too happy about."

"Such as?" I'm now concerned by the look on her face.

Her face lights up before answering, "Edward has asked me to marry him," she smiles.

"Mom that's awesome! I'm happy for you. Why do you look sad about it?"

"I'm not about that. I basically live there now, anyway, but when we make it official I'll be selling the house. I'm so sorry."

My smile quickly fades. I know I should be very happy right now. My mom deserves happiness. I will no longer have a place to live, though. "When are you thinking of selling it?"

"Well, we were thinking of getting married this summer. I am going to hire someone to do a few more updates to the house and put it on the market in a few months."

"Okay. I have a few months to figure this out. It will be fine," I smile, trying to show her I'm okay with this. Inside, I'm freaking out.

"Ms. Phillips, what are you wanting to update in your house?" The business side of Alex has come out now.

"Please, call me Janis," she smiles warmly. "I have recently had the kitchen and bathrooms redone. I was thinking of removing the popcorn ceilings, fresh paint throughout, and maybe new wood throughout, if I can find a good price for everything."

"I could come by and give you an estimate, if you'd like? I have great references and some great crews to do the job. It shouldn't take too long to complete." I pretend to follow along as they discuss what needs to be done. But deep down, I'm freaking out and want it to take longer, for my own selfish reasons. I have to find a place to live ,and with me about to start school and not making much money right now, it's gonna be hard. Dammit, Alex, why does he have to be in construction?

I'm kind of in a zone through the rest of the meal. Mom and Alex seem to be just fine now talking about her renovation plans. They are both looking at me and I hadn't realized they asked me something.

Mom tilts her head, "Jessa are you okay? Did you hear me?"

"Sorry, what was it?" Shaking my head. Alex is looking at me concerned.

"If Alex comes by tomorrow afternoon, will you be at the house?"

"Yeah, sure. I'll be there."

"Perfect. Thank you, Alex," she stands and shakes his hand. "I may have been wrong about you. Sorry again for the hard time earlier." She leans over to hug me. I don't stand, but I manage a smile, "I love you mom, and congratulations."

She offers to pay and Alex refuses to allow her. She smiles. "Thanks for dinner. I'll see you soon, honey, and Alex let me know what you come up with."

As she walks out the waitress comes by. "Can I have another apple Crown and cranberry, please?"

Alex furrows his brows at me, "Are you okay? You've been a little quiet for a while."

"I'm fine," I lie. I don't want him to know I'll soon be homeless, if I don't hurry up and get my shit together.

"Are you upset your mom's getting married?"

"No. Edward's a great guy." I'm just gonna say it. "I'm worried I won't have a place to live. Do you think you can drag out the renovations for about six months or until I find a roommate?" I'm not even joking but I smile.

He doesn't look pleased by that at all. "A roommate?" I laugh awkwardly.

"Well, yes. I can't afford to live by myself right now. I can save money until it's time to move out but even if I do it won't be enough to pay all the bills each month by myself," I sigh. Right when I thought things were looking up this happens. I really am happy for my mom I'm just worried and being selfish. I will figure it out.

"I can help you, if you want me too?"

He's so sweet. "I couldn't ask you to do that."

"You didn't. I offered. There's a big difference," he

smiles.

"You're sweet, and please don't take this the wrong way, but I really need to try and do this on my own."

"I completely understand. Now, can we leave and maybe I can help take your mind off of it for a while?" He's wiggling his eyebrows and it makes me crack up laughing, and yet again attention is drawn to our table. I don't care. He makes me laugh even when I don't want to.

"What did you have in mind? I may be persuaded."

He leans in closer and whispers, "I can show you, better than I can tell you." He takes my hand and we stand. He tosses a few bills on the table before leading me out to his truck.

CHAPTER TEN

We make it back to his house and I'm no longer thinking about my predicament. I almost forget that Alex said he was falling in love with me. I am so relieved and happy.

"Do you want something to drink before we go upstairs?"

"Nope. I'm good," I say, running up the stairs past him, causing him to laugh and hurry after me. He catches me just before we reach his door and lifts me in his arms.

"Jessa, I'm sorry I said that I was falling in love with you like that. Your mom was getting under my skin and I felt she needed to know. I had it all planned that I would tell you when we were actually alone and maybe even in bed." He starts kissing down my neck with me pressed against the door.

"I would have liked that, but I understand why you did it. She needed to know how we feel about each other. The look on her face was priceless," I laugh and Alex smiles.

"I'm going to make it up to you," he says.

He carries me into the bedroom and gently sets me on

the bed. He takes off my shirt and kisses my neck, moving down to my shoulder. I raise up so he can take my jeans and thong off. As they come off, he kisses my stomach. He looks up at me with his smoldering eyes and draws me in for a kiss, wrapping an arm around my neck and the other around my waist. He's not wearing any boxers tonight. I lift my eyebrows in surprise. I bring my hands under his shirt, running it up his chest, lifting his shirt over his head. Now we're even.

I want him naked, too. It's not fair that I am and he's still fully dressed. I reach for the button on his jeans and help him out of them.

"I'm thirsty," he says, causing me to laugh.

"You just asked me if I was and now you are," I say, looking at him silly.

"I'm thirsty. For you," he says with a growl, licking his lips, my eyes on his tongue as he teases me.

He gently pushes me back. He seems different tonight, not as intense. I like it, but also like it when he's rough. He's looking at me with a playful gleam in his eyes, causing me to smile and then a moan escapes when he licks me from my clit to my core in one swipe. He does that a few more times and puts his thumb over my entrance and circles around my arousal. I'm extremely wet and ready for him to be inside me. He pushes his thumb inside, wiggling it while sucking on my clit. It feels so good. I'm starting to tremble and buck into his hand. He removes his thumb and I groan. "Please, Alex,"

"What, Jessa? What is it?" He's teasing me now. He starts circling again and inserts two fingers while sucking my clit again. I fucking love it. He looks up at me, still pumping his fingers and I'm a panting mess. He puts his pinky from his other hand in his mouth and I'm not sure what he's going to do with it. I don't think any more fingers will fit inside me and I don't want him to try. As I'm about to protest he puts his mouth back over me and I cry out. He then slowly moves his wet finger to an unknown territory, lightly circling the tight hole.

The feeling is foreign, but it feels good. I'm now so close, with his mouth on me and his fingers inside and now this new feeling it's so overwhelming; until he slowly pushes inside. All of this is too much. I scream with pleasure, calling his name. "Oh my God, Alex." He chuckles and I feel like there's fireworks going off inside my blood. It's like nothing I've ever felt before. My body is trembling as I come down from all the sensations.

He slides up my body and rests his arms on each side of my head, looking deep into my eyes before kissing me with such passion and love that a tear rolls down my cheek.

"I love you, Jessa," he whispers before wiping the tear off my cheek.

I'm smiling so big my face hurts. "I love you, too," I whisper. I feel like I could cry. I've never felt like this before, hearing those three little words. They mean so much, hearing him say them. My heart feels whole again. I didn't realize until now how empty I'd felt inside for so long.

Using one arm to support himself above me, his other hand rakes lightly down my body leaving goosebumps and causing me to shiver until he's holding himself at my entrance. He slowly enters me, causing us both to moan. It's so good; feeling him fill me after his fingers were there moments ago. Each thrust goes deeper inside of me. He's now all the way inside and pauses looking down on me. He's fighting the urge to fuck me.

"What's wrong?"

"I don't want to fuck you. I want to make love to you," he says, kissing my lips softly. I feel my eyes welling up with tears again. I'm trying to blink them away, but all the emotions, sensations and things he's saying and showing me are so overwhelming. I've never felt love like this before. Looking back, I don't think I've ever experienced real love.

He pushes forward slowly and I can see the love in his eyes.

"I love you, Alex," I confirm what I see in his eyes.

"I love you too, Jessa. So much."

He picks up his pace a bit and kisses me, using his tongue to get past my lips. I open for him, our tongues exploring. He takes his hand and begins rubbing my clit. My heavy breaths are now turning into pants and moans. Watching him above me, seeing his muscles contract as he moves this slowly is spellbinding. I look down and see him playing with my clit and moving inside me, my arousal glistening all over his length. It's so fucking hot causing me to moan loudly. He sees me looking and does the same. I can feel my orgasm building.

He moans, "Jessa, you feel so fucking good." Hearing him moan is exhilarating and I tremble and explode around him, screaming his name. He feels me clenching around him and he begins moving faster chasing his release.

"Oh, Jessa. Fuck. It's so," he can't continue. His orgasm rockets through him and a loud moan erupts from his mouth. I feel the warmth of his orgasm inside me as he comes to a stop, staying inside.

We're both breathing heavily, both satisfied. I enjoy him making love to me. This is a different side of him that I haven't seen yet. I love all of him.

"Alex, that was just, wow!" I have no words.

"It was," he sighs.

He goes to the bathroom and washes his hands and returns with a warm wash cloth to clean me up. He's so gentle in doing so. I watch his beautiful face as he's concentrating on the task. The warm cloth feels so nice against my sensitive skin.

We lie in bed together for a while. He tickles along my naked body and it's so relaxing.

"Jessa, do you still want to work for me? I will understand if you don't."

"Yes I do, if you're okay with it? With mom selling the house I need to save all the money I can right now," I sigh. I had forgotten about all that for a bit and now I'm back to worrying again.

"I said I'd help you, Jessa, and I meant it."

"I'm very appreciative, Alex, but I need to do this for myself right now," I say, giving him a small smile. "I'm going to enroll in school after I finish here Monday. I'm excited about that."

"From what your mom said, I think it will only take a few weeks for the renovations to be complete. Do you have a plan?"

"I just found out tonight and then you said you loved me, so I hadn't really thought about it anymore after that. You've had me preoccupied," I smile.

"Do you want to stay here tonight and I'll bring you home tomorrow when I look at your mom's house?"

"That sounds nice," I say, snuggling into his side.

With all the events tonight I am emotionally and physically worn out. Alex has me wrapped in his arms. Alex had asked me what my plan was. I do need to think about that, even though I don't want to. It scares me, not knowing what my future will bring. I'm going to take it one day at a time. Since I've been living with my mom and I paid my car off a couple of years ago, I don't have any bills. I need to save every penny working for Alex. In a few weeks, I'll have some money saved, business classes behind me and can find a better job and maybe even keep working for Alex. That will be my plan for now. I'm not going to worry. The man wrapped around me makes me feel loved, happy, and safe. I will be okay.

CHAPTER ELEVEN

It's now finally Monday. Alex is going out of town for a couple of days to check on a job in Tennessee so I don't have his house today. I'm a bit disappointed I won't see him, but we had a great weekend together and the space will be good for us.

Now I am on the school site deciding what I should do. There are classes online and some I can go to on Tuesdays and Wednesdays and start new classes tomorrow. I could continue working for Alex on Mondays and Thursdays.

After contemplating, I finally make my decision. I'm now officially enrolled and go to my first class tomorrow at nine. I'm nervous. I haven't been in school in a few years now. I don't know what to expect when I get there. I want to call Alex, but I don't want to bother him at work. I'll text Brittany. She will be excited for me and hopefully ease some of this tension for me. I haven't talked to her much.

Hey girl! I'm starting class tomorrow.

That's great! Sorry I haven't called. I've been

so busy at work lately and you're so busy on top of my uncle Lol!

Ha Ha very funny. Wanna get lunch or something later?

I wish I could. I brought my lunch today knowing I wouldn't have time to leave.

You work too hard.

Tell me about it. I need help here. I gotta go. One of the salesman just walked in. He gets on my last nerve. I have enough to do right now.

Ok. Maybe we can get together soon.

The rest of the day is boring. I don't like not having anything to keep me busy. I do some cleaning and laundry and sit down with a book. Since being with Alex, I haven't had much time to read lately. I'm not complaining, but reading helps relax me and brings me into someone else's drama for a change. I can't help but letting my mind wonder, thinking about what tomorrow will be like. I wish Alex was here to take my mind off it. This book isn't helping much. I sent him a text earlier, but haven't gotten a response yet. I'm sure he's just busy.

The doorbell rings a little after seven. I look through the peep hole and can't see who it is. It kind of worries me, since I'm here by myself.

When I open the door, all I can see are roses. When they're finally lowered, I see a face I didn't expect to see. Alex's eyes are twinkling in the moonlight and he has a warm smile across his face.

"What are you doing here?" I pull him in and plant a kiss on his lips. I didn't think it through. I get poked by a few thorns in the process.

"I wanted to hurry back to see you. Is anyone here," he asks looking past me.

"Nope. It's just us," I smile mischievously. "Thank you for the flowers. They're beautiful."

He sets the roses on the entry table and lifts me into his arms. I wrap my legs around his waist as he walks me to the living room, laying me on the couch.

"Is it bad that I couldn't wait to get back to do this?" he asks, between kisses.

"No. I was just thinking about you, wishing you were here."

"Oh yeah? So, I could do what?"

"Help calm me down and not think. I was nervous about school. I start tomorrow."

"I'm here now, baby. What can I do to help relax you?"

"You're doing it," I moan arching into him.

A while later, we're still laying on the couch together. He's running his fingers through my hair and down my back. My head is resting on his shoulder. I can hear his heart beating and I feel more relaxed, and a little tired.

"How is the job going?"

"It's great. They're ahead of schedule. Should be finished by Thursday. I'll have to go back Friday, just to finish up the paperwork."

"You're leaving me again?" I say sadly, looking up at him. I'm joking, though.

"Actually, I wanted to see if you wanted to come with me. We could get away for the weekend and have some fun. Memphis isn't too far from the job."

"That sounds wonderful. Is it pathetic that I've never been to Tennessee?" I ask, scrunching up my face. "I do need to see how the classes go, though, in case I have homework or need to study."

"I understand. Tennessee is a lot of fun. There's a lot of live music, bars and restaurants down Beale Street. I don't like staying out too late though. It gets very crowded and can get sort of chaotic."

"How are you okay being in huge crowds there, but basically stay home all the time?" I'm confused.

He sighs, "No one knows me there. Everyone knows me here. You see how your mom reacted at first the other night."

"Yes, and you also see that what she thought was wrong

and she even apologized. You need to allow people to see you, so they can get to know you and know that you're not the monster you were made out to be. They only know the rumors from the case, Alex. I didn't know any of it. Not everyone in this freaking town does." I'm slightly agitated. I want him to just deal with it and move on. I want him to move on with me.

Alex chuckles, "You were younger, Jessa. You didn't keep up with the news I'm sure."

"I didn't and I still don't. It's depressing. Can you please just try?"

"I've gotten so used to being in this bubble. It's my comfort zone. Ya know?"

"I get that, but for us to work, Alex, I won't be in a bubble forever." I look up, searching his face trying to see what he's thinking. He looks guarded, but his face softens and he caresses my cheek.

"I'll do anything to be with you, Jessa. I love you. You said forever. Do you see us being together, forever?"

I smile, "I do. I could, but you must quit allowing yourself to be like this. It's not healthy. I was thinking of a way that could help change people's perception of you, even though it doesn't matter. What do you think about donating to a battered woman's shelter or maybe starting your own charity for women or something like that?"

"That sounds like a great idea. I just don't want a lot of exposure from it," he frowns.

"That's kind of the point of it. I want people to see what I see in you. You're an amazing person."

"Why couldn't I have met you first?" He shakes his head taking a deep breath then kissing me as if it would be our last. He does that a lot and it worries me that he doesn't think we can last through all of this. Only we can, if he will try and let me help him.

"Alex, I may not have been your first love, but I want to be the last. Please, just let me help you." I feel a tear fall. I don't want to cry about this but I want him to deal with this. He can't continue living like this.

"Okay." He wipes the tear away. "Please don't be upset. We can talk more about it soon. Let's go upstairs to bed. You need a good night's sleep to be ready for your first day of school tomorrow. I don't know why that sounded so creepy saying that." He laughs and then carries me up to bed.

Alex helps me get through the night, not stressing about school, but I now keep thinking about him and how he lives his life of solitude. It's such a sad situation and I hope I can help him through it. If he doesn't I'm afraid we won't be able to stay together. It's not healthy.

CHAPTER TWELVE

I wake up to the smell of bacon. I throw on Alex's shirt and hurry downstairs. When I reach the kitchen, I stop at the sight. Alex is facing the stove in his boxers, stirring something. Seeing his toned back muscles moving as he stirs is such a great thing to see first thing in the morning. It's so hot, seeing your man cooking for you.

I sneak up behind him before he notices me and kiss his shoulder. I startle him and he jumps, stepping backwards right on my toes.

"Ow." I hop back. "That wasn't how I saw that going in my head."

"I'm sorry. Are you okay?" His eyes skim back up my body to my hair, mangled around my face. When he looks me over like that I feel so anxious, and turned on at the same time. My body feels like it heats as his eyes roam over me.

"You look really hot in my t-shirt," he says, wrapping his arms around me, coming in for a kiss. I cover my mouth quickly and he furrows his brows.

"I haven't brushed my teeth yet," I giggle stepping around him. "You're about to burn the bacon."

"Shit!" When he flips, it pops and he jumps in front of me to block the grease from hitting me. He instantly hisses.

"Are you okay?" I ask concerned.

He chuckles turning to face me, "I'm a man, Jessa. A little grease can't hurt me." He quickly steals a kiss and then wears a triumphant smile. "I wanted to make you breakfast before school. My mom always said it was the most important meal of the day, but seeing you in my shirt, I think she may have been wrong."

Alex kisses me goodbye and wishes me luck. We plan on dinner tonight so I can tell him about my first day.

I get in my car with a smile. When he's gone from view my smile instantly falls. I'm so nervous. I wish he could come with me. That basically ruins any of my plans to feel more independent and not be so consumed by a man, by him, but he makes it so hard. I wish he could see himself the way I do.

I pull in the parking lot and it is basically full. I find a couple of spots all the way in the back, lucky me. I sit here, taking a few deep breaths before getting out and heading inside. I feel like this is the first day of high school all over again, only then I had Amber with me. I wasn't alone. I need to get over myself and just do this. I'll be fine. I just have a weird feeling. I guess it's the newness and the not knowing what's going to happen.

I walk through the doors and there are people buzzing around with backpacks and laptop cases, knowing exactly where they need to go. I see a sign on the wall the has arrows pointing in different directions. I see the arrow for the office and walk that way.

I walk in and there's a little old lady with glasses in a floral dress smiling as I walk in.

"Hello! How can I help you?"

"Hi. This is my first day. I'm Jessa Phillips, taking the business class."

"Okay. Let me print out your schedule for you and you'll be all set," she smiles warmly.

"Thank you." I watch her walk away briefly, returning with my schedule.

"Here ya go. Have a great first day and if you have any questions feel free to come back and ask me." I wish I could be as happy as she is to be here. I know this is going to help me so much with finding a career. I just need to get this first day behind me and I'll feel a lot better.

After walking down a long hallway with many doors I finally find my classroom. One more deep breath before I open the door and walk inside. I scan the room and many of the students stop and look at me, going right back to their conversations as if I wasn't there. The teacher isn't here, yet, so I walk to the back of the class and take the only seat left.

I scan the room and see a girl who looks familiar. I can't place her name, but I know we went to school together. We weren't friends, though. I think we may have had a couple of classes together. She catches me looking at her. I probably look like a moron staring, but it's bugging me what her name is. She smiles, so I guess I didn't freak her out. I smile in return as the door opens. Holy shit! The teacher looks like he missed his calling. He's really cute. It shouldn't be too hard to pay attention in this class at all.

He walks in and smiles. His eyes land on me and he smiles wider.

"Hello. You're new. Welcome to the class." I smile, not saying a word. I don't want all this attention to stay focused on me. He passes out a few papers for us to look over for a quiz before the end of class.

I think I did well. After a couple of hours in here it's now time for a thirty-minute lunch break before my next class. I am quite hungry. I hope the food is better here than it was in high school.

I follow the signs for the food court and after a few halls and turns to the right I find it. I could get lost here. It's bigger than I imagined. Looking around, I'm grateful there are a few options to eat. The setup is very similar to the food court in the mall. There's a spot with pizza, another with different kinds of sandwiches, a salad bar, and finally, a Starbucks. Thank God.

I decide on a turkey sandwich with a sweet tea to drink. I find an unoccupied table and sit facing the rest of the area so I can people watch. There's a good hundred or so people in seats or in lines, chatting and eating their lunches. Mine actually tastes good. I'm surprised for school food, but we're not kids anymore so they have to up the flavor, I guess.

When I'm almost finished, I see the girl from class that I can't remember heading towards me.

"You're Jessa, right?"

"Yes. You look very familiar. We went to school together, didn't we?"

"I think we had civics together in ninth grade. I'm Julie," she says, taking a seat across from me. "So, I heard about Amber and Tyler." Wow! She didn't waste any time fishing for gossip.

"Yeah. It is what it is." I'm not giving her any details. "It's all for the best. I've found a great man. He's amazing."

"That's great. Did you know Tyler also goes here?" My face falls with this information.

"No I didn't. What's he taking? How not to be a cheating douchebag?"

She laughs. "I think he's taking a business class and a culinary class. Maybe more. I'm not too sure."

"I hope he's not in my next class with me, then," I frown, pulling out my schedule.

"I hate to break it to you but he is in that class with us. I also have it."

"Fuck," I say, looking at her quickly. "Sorry."

"You're fine, really. I heard it all and have probably said more."

Lunch is over. Julie and I walk to our next class together. She seems nice enough. We weren't friends in high school. She was a real bookworm type. She's small, very pale and has glasses. I think she could be gorgeous if she tried. I don't think she cares, though. I'm glad she's walking with me and knows where she's going. The closer we get to the class, the more bitter I become. I do not want to see him. I'm not sure what I might do. I don't want to make a fool of myself or seem like the crazy girl in school.

Julie stops at the door turning towards me and smiles sweetly.

"You can sit by me if you want. There aren't desks. We sit two to a table. I never have anyone sitting with me," she looks to the floor, embarrassed.

"That would be great. Thank you so much."

We walk in and I instantly feel his eyes on me, and it sickens me. I want to scratch his eyes out and I haven't even seen him, yet. I look straight ahead, following Julie to the table.

"Did you see him staring at you?" she whispers.

"I tried not to see where he was, but I could feel it."

"Well he's right in front of you." I look up and as I do he turns around.

"Hey, Jessa," he says a bit nervously. He's smiling and I want to knock his teeth down his throat. I don't reply. I act like I didn't even hear him and open my notebook and retrieve my pen, getting ready for class to begin. He's making me very uncomfortable. He's still watching me.

Our teacher walks in and he looks like Colonel Sanders. He passes out a few papers for us to complete in class and that keeps Tyler from bothering me. He also gives us an assignment for homework. It's based on where we see ourselves in five years. I think it will be fun, and it makes me think of Alex.

"What's got you smiling?"

I'm pulled from my thoughts and realize Tyler is speaking to me and my face falls.

"My boyfriend, actually." I say rudely.

"Oh. You're still with that guy?"

"Yes, I am, and he's great."

"Huh," he says, turning around.

The class ends and shortly after Julie and I reach her car.

"Thanks a lot, for letting me sit with you. You have no idea how much you helped me through this day."

"No problem. It was nice to have someone sit with me." I feel bad for her. She seems very lonely and she seems quiet, most of the time. I'll have to invite her over or maybe we can go out sometime. I think we could be friends.

I wave and start towards my car, all the way in the back of the lot. I can hear someone coming up behind me and I know it's Tyler. I'm not turning around to check.

"Jessa, wait up," he says trying to catch his breath as he comes up beside me.

"What do you want, Tyler?" I sigh, turning towards him, waiting to hear the bullshit that's about to fall out of his mouth.

"Do you have time to go for coffee and maybe talk for a few minutes?"

"No. I don't, and even if I did, I don't want to spend any time with you."

"Because of him?" He now has an attitude.

"Um. Even if I didn't have Alex I wouldn't want anything to do with you. You fucked my best friend in our bed. That's not something you get over, or even want to. I'm done." I reach for my door handle and he grabs my arm spinning me around to look at him. I'm in total shock that he put his hands on me. I jerk away, but he holds my arm tighter.

"Let go of me!" I yell.

He looks around, making sure I hadn't drawn attention to us. Being in the back of the parking lot, where most of the teachers park ,there's no one around.

"You really think he can make you as happy as we were?" I laugh and I can see the anger building all over his face that's now turning red.

"He has showed me how unhappy I really was with you. Not that it's any of your business, but he is caring, loving and treats me with respect."

"I did all of those things," he says furiously.

"Oh really? Fucking my best friend kind of proves differently." I shake my head and try to get out of his grasp. He doesn't let up and he's hurting me.

"That was one time. I'll never do it again. I made a

mistake and I'm trying to fix it. Please let me?" He lets go of my arm and his face has changed to one of regret.

"It's too late for that, Tyler." I turn and quickly get in my car, locking the doors. He's standing there, looking at me and the anger is building again.

"I won't give up," he yells before punching the hood of my car.

"You're an asshole and I want nothing to do with you. Leave me alone," I scream before speeding away.

On the drive home, I think of how crazy Tyler was acting. My arm still hurts. He's never laid a hand on me before. I don't know what has come over him. He's never made me feel scared. Ever. Is it because I've moved on? Does he realize he's lost any chance of being with me? I don't know, but he'd better never touch me again. I hope it doesn't leave a bruise, because if Alex sees it and he asks, I won't lie to him. I'm not bringing it up though. He has enough to deal with on his own to have something like this as a distraction or an excuse to get out of working on himself. I can handle Tyler on my own.

CHAPTER THIRTEEN

Alex is picking me up in fifteen minutes. He's made dinner for me. Since we're eating in, I pick jeans and a long-sleeve shirt to cover my bruising arm. There's only one way he'll see it and that's only if he gets me naked. I want him too, but I don't want to ruin our night discussing Tyler. Maybe I can manage to keep my shirt on.

Alex arrives early, as usual. He has a huge smile on his face as I open the door.

"How was your first day?" He seems excited to hear about my day.

"School was good," I say, trying to sound convincing. He doesn't buy it at all.

"What happened?" he asks concerned.

"You'll never guess who's in one of my classes?"

"I don't know who? Wait. No! The ex?"

"Ding. Ding. Ding," I sigh. Alex doesn't seem happy about this at all.

He frowns. "Did he bother you?"

"He did, but I handled it. He's just mad that you and I are still together and that I won't take him back," I say, leaning in for a kiss. I press myself into him to try and get his mind off Tyler because I don't want to think about him anymore tonight. I want to have a nice evening with Alex.

It worked. He moans into my mouth and I feel him hardening against my stomach.

"Let's go before I have my dessert first."

I grab my purse and keys from the table as we walk out and I close the door behind me, locking it and following Alex to his truck. He opens my door and helps me inside before walking around to the driver's side. He looks at me before starting the truck. "Jessa I know you said you handled it, but please, tell me if he does anything to make you uncomfortable."

"I will," I say, looking out the window. I hate that I didn't tell him what happened. I don't need him helping me with this. Tyler can fuck off.

Alex is a great cook. I shouldn't be surprised. He's good at everything he does. He's prepared a delicious chicken alfredo and homemade garlic bread. He makes our plates and a glass of wine for me. He grabs a beer out of the fridge for himself before sitting with me.

We enjoy our meal and I tell him about my day.

"I even have homework so I can't stay too long," I crinkle my face and he smiles.

"Anything I can help you with?"

"It's basically a report about each level of a business.

Each role and what it contributes to a company. If you don't mind, I'd like to use yours as my example?"

"That would be great," he smiles.

After we finish the wonderful dinner Alex made we sit on the couch and he gives me a rundown of all the employees and what they do for his company.

"Poor Brittany has so much on her plate. I think you need to go in more often to help her."

Alex sighs, "You know why I don't."

"Yes, I do, but do you think if your employees hated you that they'd be working for you?"

He thinks about it. "I don't know. I guess not."

"I really think a lot of this is all in your head. With you being found innocent, I don't believe people think of you the way you think they do."

"You weren't there. You didn't hear the gasps and the dirty looks I got for months after."

"No, I wasn't there. So, basically your personal life was revealed. You and Lizzy weren't faithful with each other. You also have preferences in the bedroom that she didn't like. Do you think you're the only one in this town that doesn't like it a little kinky? I mean, come on."

"Lizzy had told her friends and her mother very personal things that she shouldn't have. They knew too much about how I like to fuck. Now, the whole town knows."

"So fucking what. Also, if supposedly everyone knows then that means that they know that I obviously like it, too, if I'm with you. Right? I don't give a fuck what people think. You shouldn't, either."

"It was humiliating. They all know that I wanted to tie her up and that I said dirty things to her and it made them think that I must have beaten her, too. After one night, I tried to get her to try it my way and she bruised. It was easy to make them think that I tried to hurt her because she wouldn't give it to me how I wanted and that she'd eventually trapped me by getting pregnant, causing me to want to kill her. This is a small town, where everyone knows everyone and all the elders talk. They don't understand anything outside of missionary." He has tears in his eyes and it makes me sad that he feels this way.

"When you do go out, do you still feel the dirty looks and whispers?" I haven't noticed any of that. It is all in his head.

He sighs looking resigned, "I don't know. I just try to keep to myself."

"I get that your sex life was made public but it's not like you're a woman beater. I love how you are in bed. A lot of women would."

He smiles sadly, "It was so hard going through all that. Lizzy and I were going to try and make it work. I was going to try and let go of my sexual needs for her. She was carrying my child. I did love her. We were going to have a new start and then it was ripped away from me so quickly. Then to be accused of beating her and then killing her because she wouldn't give me what I wanted or how I wanted it. I had such a hard time with losing her and our child I'll never know, never hold and to then be made to look like such a monster. I didn't even have a chance to grieve for them."

"I'm sorry, Alex. I want to help you through this, but you must try to stop caring what others think. It's the only way to move on. You've been punishing yourself for no reason. You didn't cause the accident."

"I know I didn't. It's just so fucked up how everything unfolded the way it did." He considers my eyes and then looks away. "I still miss her, Jessa."

"Of course you do. She was your wife."

"I feel guilty for loving you. I don't know why." He buries his face in his hands.

I'm not sure what to say to that. He and Lizzy were together for years. I know it must feel weird, being with someone new after all that time being with her. I just want him to be happy. Happy with me. I don't want him to feel guilty.

"I love you, Alex. I would never ask you to forget your time with Lizzy. I just see how unhealthy it is for you blaming yourself for everything and what everyone thinks. And not everyone feels the way you think they do. I just want you to try and see it. I want you to see that you're not a bad person in everyone's eyes, especially mine." I wrap my arms around him squeezing a bit too tight.

He groans, "Are you trying to squeeze me to death?" He

looks up and smiles sweetly. "I love you, too, Jessa. I'm so lucky to have you."

That's what I want. I don't want him torturing himself anymore.

"Wanna start back on your report?"

"Sure." I grab my papers off the coffee table. "I'm to sales now."

Alex finishes giving me information about his company and I help clean up from dinner and then he drives me home. He was somewhat distant after our conversation. I hope it doesn't affect his progress. I'm trying so hard to help him move forward. With me.

Now, I'm lying in bed, thinking about my day. It was a crazy, to say the least. Tyler had better not talk to me or ever touch me again. He scared me with how he acted today. I've never seen him like that before. He's never been physical with me in all the years we were together. He better be glad I didn't tell Alex about it. I'm not sure what Alex would have done. I don't want to find out, either.

I feel a lot better walking into school this morning. I haven't seen Tyler and I'm glad. I'm sure he's lurking around somewhere. I see Julie and wave, walking towards her.

"Hi!"

"Hi, Jessa! Want to walk to class together?"

"Sure," I smile.

"Did you get the report finished last night?"

"I did. I used my boyfriend's business as my example. How about you?"

"Yes. I used the company my dad works for."

We take a lot of notes in our first class. It seems to go by fast. We stay very busy, compared to the second one. It's a bit more laid back and there's more interaction with each other. I like that about it.

Julie and I have lunch together, chatting about class. I still haven't seen Tyler. It's a good thing too. I enjoyed my lunch and I want to keep it down.

We walk into our next class and I see Tyler sitting at the table in front of ours, looking at his phone. He looks weird. He's pale and seems tired. Maybe he stayed up too late playing video games, or maybe he's sick. The later makes me smile. I hope he has a stomach bug.

He glares at me and I act like I don't notice him as I walk past him and take my seat.

Julie turns to me, "What's your boyfriend's business?"

"He owns a construction company not too far from here. It's doing very well."

Julie smiles and looks at the back of Tyler's head. I shake my head, knowing exactly what she's doing and can't help but grin at her attempt to make him jealous.

We each had to present our report of the businesses we chose. I think I did well. I wasn't shocked that Tyler used his mother's daycare for his report. She probably did it for him.

My phone dings with a text message from Alex, instantly causing me to smile. He's asking me to meet him at his office after school. I'm a bit shocked he's there. I send a text back and now I can't wait for the bell to ring so I can see him. I hope everything's okay.

CHAPTER FOURTEEN

I pull in to the parking lot and get out. Closing my door, I feel like something's off. Something is not right. I scan the parking lot and see nothing other than a couple of company trucks on one side. Alex's and Brittany's are on the other. I look at the street and see what looks like Tyler's car parked across the street. I start walking toward the road, to enter the front of the building and see it is Tyler, and he's watching me. He looks angry and then speeds away. Did he follow me? Is he stalking me now? What the hell? I don't know what I should do. Should I tell Alex? Now Tyler knows where Alex works. I don't know how I feel about that.

I try to shake the weird feeling and walk in; I smile when I see Brittany at her desk.

"Holy shit. Your desk looks like a tornado hit it."

"Tell me about it. I need some organizing," she says, wiggling her eyes. "Do you know anyone?"

"I do and she's awesome," I brag, causing Brittany to laugh.

"What are you doing here?"

"Alex asked me to come after school. Is everything

okay?"

"Yes. Fine. I'm not sure why he's here. It was a shock to me. He grabbed a couple stacks of files from my desk and has been in his office ever since." She shrugged her shoulders.

"You mean there was actually more clutter on your desk?" She flips me off and laughs.

"I really will help you, if you want me to?"

"That would be great. Alex's office is right down there, to the left." She points down the hall.

"Thanks. I'll be back soon to help with this chaos." I wave my hands above her desk. I'm sure it's under there somewhere.

I knock on Alex's door. "Come in."

I open the door and he smiles, getting up from his desk and walking around it to greet me. He seems happy. "Everything oka?" I kiss him.

"Yes. Someone helped me see I need to get past my fears and I need to be a bigger part of my company. You should've seen Brittany's face when I walked in," he laughs.

"That must be a smart person you're listening to."

"Oh, she is very smart and beautiful too." He kisses me. I open for him, his tongue dipping inside, meeting my own. He presses himself against me, holding me close. I pull away to catch my breath, searching his face. "You sure are happy today. I'm so proud of you."

"I thought a lot about what you said last night. When I came in today and saw Brittany's desk, I realized I hadn't been fair to her, my company, or you. I want to do better. I want to overcome all these fears I have."

"You have no idea how happy that makes me, to hear you say that. I'm so proud of you. I love you," I crush my mouth to his.

"I love you, too," he mumbles between my lips, pushing me against the door and pressing himself into me. I can feel that he wants me. I moan into his mouth.

"Um. We're in your office," I whisper.

"Why are you whispering?" he laughs.

"I don't know. Brittany is here."

"She's up front, working. I haven't seen her since I walked in this morning. She's busy anyway." He says, lifting my shirt over my head.

"I don't know. What if she hears us?"

"I guess we'll have to be quiet, won't we?" He wiggles his eyebrows. He looks so silly when he does it and I love it.

I'm contemplating what to do when he drops to his knees. He pulls my jeans and panties down with one fast tug, causing me to gasp. I cover my mouth quickly. Seeing him on his knees in front of me does me in. He looks up at me for permission. I can't deny him. It's too late now. I want it. I want his tongue on me. He can by the arousal in my eyes that he's won. He smiles licking his lips before he kisses my pelvic bone. I grab his hair, pulling him closer to me. He looks up at me and licks from my entrance all the way up to the top of my clit where he had just kissed me. My head falls back against the door and my eyes close. He grips my ass, pulling me away from the door. He stands and I whimper.

"I can be quiet," I plead.

He leads the way and gently pushes me backwards until I'm lying on his cold desk. My back instantly arches. He kneels again and licks me like I'm an ice cream cone, melting in one-hundred-degree weather. I'm biting my bottom lip, trying not to be loud. It's hard to be quiet. I don't like it. I want to focus on the pleasure he's giving me, but I'm too worried Brittany, or someone else, will hear us... well, me.

I'm so close. A few more strokes and I feel my legs begin to shake. He places his tongue firmly over my clit and sucks. I bite my lip so hard I can taste blood as my orgasm slams through me. He's holding my legs apart licking lightly as I fall back down.

Alex stands, wiping his mouth on his dress shirt and winks at me. I can't move. My legs feel like Jell-O. I'm still panting, trying to catch my breath.

"You look so sexy, naked and spread out on my desk. I will take a mental picture of this and imagine you there each morning.

"You're going to come in every day now?" I smile, waiting for his reply. He hadn't realized what he'd said, I guess.

"Yes. I think I should. It is my company and I need to be present and more involved," he nods as if he's telling himself, and not just me. "Baby, your lips are bleeding." I start to look around for a tissue, when he leans forward, kissing me hard. He finally pulls back, and I am panting. He smirks, "All gone now."

"How else was I going to be quiet?" I wipe my lips a few times smiling. "So, is this why I was summoned to come here?" Pun intended, I wink.

"I was working, and it actually felt good to be back here. That got me to thinking about why I needed to be here." He took a moment to compose his thoughts. "It was you, and everything you'd said last night. You were right, I needed to face my fears. Nathan, who's in sales came in. He was confused at first, because my light was on, and he came in to see why." He shook his head and laughed. "He said he was shocked as shit to actually see me here in the flesh. I told him why, I was basically a ghost here, and he ended up saying a lot of the same things you did.

"He sounds like a smart guy," I smile getting my clothes back on. Alex watches my every movement.

"He is. He's very good at his job. We had become good friends until everything happened. You know how guys are. We're not all mushy, and never talk about feelings, so he gave me my space, and we kept things professional."

A knock at the door has me scurrying to finish getting dressed. I hastily button my jeans and run my fingers through my hair, so it looks semi-presentable. Alex looks me over and nods. I nod back and smile, embarrassed.

"Come in."

Brittany strolls in. "What's going on?" Brittany takes one look at the both of us and holds up her hands, "Never mind. Don't tell me. I don't wanna know." She drops a file on Alex's desk. "Here's the Peterson's material order for you to sign off on for Friday. If you sign it before you leave, I can fax it back over before the end of the day." She gives me a wink on her way out the door. "Oh, and brush the back of your hair," she yells over her shoulder right before she shuts the door. I turn around feeling the heat in my face. Alex is fucking laughing.

"What the fuck's so funny," I ask already knowing.

He shakes his head, still laughing. "You are adorable when you're embarrassed."

I cross my arms and huff, showing him my best pouty look. He walks towards me, giving me a chaste kiss. And just like that, I forget what I was pouting about.

I run my fingers through my hair again, as I headed for the door, I say, "I'm going to help Brittany organize her desk now. I hope I can find one under there."

"Okay. I've noticed a lot of stuff that could be organized better, if you'd like to help me out sometime and I'll pay you for it?"

"How will you pay me exactly?" I put my hand on his thigh and rub my way up to the crotch giving him a little pat. He's still hard. I must admit, it makes me happy to know I'm leaving him like this, unsatisfied after making fun of me. I sashay right out the door and don't look back. I do hear him groan and his chair squeaking. He must be trying to adjust himself. I smile and giggle as I make my way to Brittany.

"Ready for me to work my magic?" Brittany jumps, seemingly, distracted. I furrow my brow. "What's wrong?"

"Look." She's points out the front door. "That car has passed by here about ten times now."

I look the way she's pointing and my eyes go wide. Fuck. It's Tyler. It just has to be. I would recognize that car anywhere. I glance back at Brittany, who still looks concerned as she stares out the window. I can't exactly tell her who it is. If I mention that Tyler is possibly looking for me, she would run to Alex so fast.

"Maybe they're lost," I say, shrugging my shoulders, hoping she gives up on it. I walk to the front of her desk, trying to focus on the task at hand, not the crazy guy outside.

"I'm going to organize these files in alphabetical order, okay?"

"Uh, yeah. Sure." She's still looking in the direction Tyler's car went, before finally paying attention to me. "Sorry. What?"

"There's this thing called a file cabinet. I was gonna put these folders in alphabetical order," I smile, waving them in her face.

"Ha, ha. Very funny. Yes, that's fine. I just haven't had time to do it. You bitch." I start laughing at her and she joins me.

An hour later, not only can we see Brittany's desk, but

Tyler hasn't driven by again. I'm still worried about what he's thinking, why he's acting like this. I never would have expected him to be such a jealous asshole.

"Holy shit!" Alex says, walking out of his office. "Jessa, you are amazing. I want you as my company organizer." I smile and he walks up for a kiss.

"Y'all stop it. You're grossing me out," Brittany says choking.

"Oh, shut your face," I laugh.

"On that note, I'm out of here. Thanks for the help Jessa. I'll see y'all over the weekend maybe?"

"Yeah. Let's go out." I look to Alex, "You coming along? We may need a strong guy to protect us," I kid, grabbing his rock-hard biceps. I'm joking, but not really, after the new stalker issues.

"Yes. I'll come. Where?"

"Who are you? What happened to my uncle? I love this new and improved one. Jessa, you have to stay with him. Marry him, if you have to." My eyes go to Alex and he's gone a bit pale. He looks at me and I give him a small smile and roll my eyes at what she'd said.

"Alex, will you walk me out? There was a car that was driving back and forth earlier and it has me feeling uneasy."

Alex immediately tenses as he walks to the door. He looks back at Brittany briefly. "How long has it been going on? What did it look like? Why didn't you say something sooner?"

She shrugs, "It's been about an hour since I last saw it." He narrows his eyes, as he looks between Brittany and I quickly dart my eyes.

He sighs, "Let's go. I'll walk y'all out." I know he can protect us, especially since the nut in question is my ex-boyfriend.

We walk out to the parking lot and I scan the road. There's no sight of Tyler and I sigh in relief.

"Bye, Brittany," I wave.

"Bye, bitch," she smiles and waves back.

I turn to Alex, "So do you want me to come clean for you tomorrow?"

"Yes, please. Do you need me to be there with you?"

"No," I laugh. "Unless you don't trust me?"

"Don't be ridiculous," he rolls his eyes and jerks me close to him. "I will go in a little late so I can let you in, though. Okay?"

"Sounds great. I love you."

"I love you, too, Jessa," he says, gripping the back of my neck and pulling me in for a passionate kiss.

I get in my car and drive home. I can't help but look in the rear-view mirror, watching for Tyler's car. There is no sign of him and I feel a little bit more at ease.

Alex surprised me today. He's taking a big step in the right direction. I'm so proud of him.

CHAPTER FIFTEEN

It's like the first day we met. Alex answers the door shirtless and I can't help but have the exact same feelings as then, only now, he's mine.

"Good morning, beautiful," he greets me, pulling me into him for a kiss.

"Good morning yourself. Dressed like that I'm not going to get much work done today," I say, eyeing the gorgeous body in front of me.

"Well that sounds like a plan," he grins, stepping aside to let me in.

"I do need to work today. It's been over a week and I want to keep your OCD at bay."

He grabs me around the waist, tickling my ribs. I scream and wiggle trying to get away from his grasp.

"Are you making fun of me?" He looks at me like he could pounce at any moment.

"Not at all. That's one of the many qualities I love about you," I say as I walk to the kitchen and set my stuff down.

"Okay. Do you need me for anything before I head to the office?"

"I could think of a few things, but no, you go to work so I can work."

"Okay. I'll see you tonight?" He asks and I nod.

He pulls me into his arms and says, "Great, because I have plans for you. Bring some clothes to stay over too. I figured since you don't have school or work tomorrow we could spend the night together and maybe do something fun tomorrow."

"That sounds great."

Alex kisses me goodbye and slaps my ass on his way out the door.

I turn on Alex's badass surround sound and jam while I clean. I can get some shit done and stay focused with the beat of the music. I've gotten the whole upstairs done already and am now sweeping my way down the stairs. My stomach starts growling and I realize I didn't pack a lunch this morning. I was in too much of a hurry to see my man. I find some lunchmeat and make a sandwich. I eat quickly and get back to work.

I'm almost finished, now. He had a lot of laundry since I missed my last cleaning when he was out of town. I finally put the last load in the dryer and start mopping my way out. As I've been cleaning, I start to notice, it's weird with him not here. I've thought a lot about him today. I want to surprise him somehow. Maybe I can buy a new outfit for the bedroom that's not too expensive. I even have a half-off coupon for the store in town. I bet he'd like that a lot. I have no idea what he would like or even what colors to choose.

I'm sitting at home on the laptop, looking at the lingerie store's website, trying to find something special for tonight. I can find what I want and then drive into town and pick it up, and not be in the store as long searching for something I want. There are so many outfits and different styles to choose from. I finally find what I'm looking for. It's a black one piece, tiny thing that looks like leather with silver studs. At the top, it starts with a studded collar that has a black strip connecting to the bra part, which is basically triangular shaped and open to have my boobs on full display. There's another strip of black that runs down the center of the stomach connecting with two holes for your legs to go through revealing an open crotch. It's very sexy. I hope he will like it. It is so out of my comfort zone. I've never wanted to wear lingerie before, but I'm excited to surprise Alex with it before bed. I search the site a bit more and under accessories they have several adult toys. I wonder if he'd be into that? I'm sure he would and decide on some black furry cuffs. I think I could really enjoy having him using them on me. I had bought a pair when I was with Tyler and he threw them away. He thought it was a stupid idea. He was never willing to try anything I wanted to try to spice up our boring sex life.

I walk into the store and a woman greets me with a smile.

"Hello! How can I help you?"

"Hi. I was on your website earlier and saw an outfit I wanted to purchase." I wasn't embarrassed when looking online. Now that I'm here, and there's all sorts of outfits hanging from the ceiling almost dangling on my head, I'm a bit mortified. I feel my face heating.

"If you need any help just let me know," she smiles.

"Thanks." I think she could tell and could probably see I was a bit embarrassed. I'm glad she's not going to follow me around like one of those annoying salespeople, trying to work for their commission.

After walking down several aisles I finally find the outfit I saw online and they even have it in my size. I didn't think about shoes and don't have the extra funds to be splurging, but with this outfit I need heels. Not super high ones, because I don't want to fall. That wouldn't be sexy at all. I go to the sale aisle and find the section with my size. I see a cute pair that aren't too high or too short. They're on sale for fifteen dollars. That's perfect. I put them in my basket and head to the accessories department. Holy shit! They have so many things and I have no idea what some of it's even used for. Some things look extremely painful. I find the black furry cuffs and walk to the checkout. I'm so glad no one else is checking out. I did see a few women shopping and I tried not to pay attention to what they were here for.

I walk out and run right into someone, dropping my bag.

"I'm so sorry," I say, picking up my bag and looking up, right into the eyes of the sleazy asshole that is Tyler.

"What did you get in there," he nods to the store, looking angry.

"That's none of your business," I say, putting the bag behind my back.

"Trying to look like a little slut for your douchebag boyfriend?" He sneers. He glares at me.

How fucking dare, he?! He is not allowed to talk to me this way. He knows exactly how to push my buttons and I'm gonna push right back.

"Actually, yes I am. I have big plans for the night," I plastered on a huge smile as I moved to walk past him.

"You know, you'd never have had to go in a place like that for me."

"Oh, I know. It was always the same with you."

"What the fuck is that supposed to mean?" He's raising his voice and people are starting to notice.

"It doesn't even matter anymore Tyler."

"Yes it fucking does matter."

I glance around me, people are starting to focus their attention on us. "Stop yelling," I hiss. "You're drawing attention to yourself."

"I don't care. Now answer the question." I'm not sure what is going on with him. He has never been this angry before, other than when he was losing on a video game. He would yell and maybe throw the remote, but right now he's acting like a lunatic.

"You do not own me. I don't have to do a damn thing you say. You're wasting my time and I have somewhere to be." I turn to leave, but stop and turn back to him. "And stop fucking stalking me. Don't think I haven't noticed. It's fucking psycho." I storm away quickly and get in my car and drive home.

As I take a shower, I can't stop thinking about how angry Tyler was and how weird and almost crazy he was. How can he be so angry with me? He's the one who fucked up. He has no right treating me that way. He really scared me today.

I finish my shower and try to push those thoughts aside. I straighten my hair and put on a little bit of makeup. I want this to be a special night for us. I try on the outfit and look at myself in the mirror. It fits well and I feel sexy in it. The bruise on my arm is barely noticeable. If Alex does notice it, I'll say I bumped into something the other day. I hope it doesn't come to that. I don't want to lie to him, but he's doing so well. I don't want to chance a setback. I put on my heels and walk around a bit to get used to them. I'm so not a heel-wearing girl.

Alex texts, letting me know he is on his way home from the office, so I quickly find a cute sweater and jeans to wear over the top. I undo the collar and tuck it into the sweater so he doesn't notice it. I want this to be a surprise and blow him away. I have this idea in my head to undress in front of him revealing the sexy little outfit. I think I'll do a shimmy and shake as I take off my clothes for him. I've never stripped for anyone and hope I don't look like a total ass.

On the drive to Alex's, I must admit I didn't think this through. The outfit is a bit uncomfortable under my clothes, especially the jeans. The garters around the tops of my thighs feel so tight right now. I squirm and wiggle trying, to no avail, to find some comfort. I now wonder what plans Alex has for the night. I'm not too sure how long I can keep my clothes on with this thing on underneath.

After what seems like a forever drive, I finally pulled into the driveway. I hop out quickly and grab my overnight tote bag and shimmy once more.

As I reach the door, Alex has an amused look on his face. "What are you doing?" He walks up behind me, wrapping his arms around me and starts kissing my neck.

"These jeans are so uncomfortable."

"I can help you out of them later, if you'd like," he grins wickedly. "I've made dinner reservations for us at Claire's."

I frown, as I look down at my jeans and sweater. "Wow! I'm so not dressed for that, though, Alex."

"You look beautiful and holy fuck me, you're wearing heels," his eyes skim down my body.

"Do you really think it's okay? I didn't know we were going anywhere." Fuck I'm going to be so uncomfortable tonight.

"I think you look amazing. Our reservation is at seven thirty. I'll turn off all the lights and we can go. The house looks great, by the way," he says, hitting a few switches and grabbing his keys.

"Thank you. Why are we going to Claire's? I mean, I think it's sweet. I'm just curious."

"Well, I'm trying to get out of my comfort zone and originally was going to order takeout," he crinkles his nose. "You've been helping me so much lately. I wanted to do something special for you."

"That's so sweet, Alex. I have a surprise for you when we get home."

"Oh yeah?"

"Yep. Hopefully you'll love it."

"Well let's get out of here so we can get back for my surprise," he says, pulling me out the door.

Claire's is a very elegant restaurant. I've only been once with my mom and her boyfriend, Edward. He surprised her for her birthday. They have white table cloths and a single rose in a tiny crystal vase on each table. They also have a pianist to set the scene. It's a beautiful restaurant with delicious food. And it's expensive.

Even though I am stuffed, that isn't going to deter me from agreeing to dessert. Alex feeds me a piece of cake. I close my eyes and moaned with approval. When I open my eyes, Alex is staring at me with a look of lust on his face.

"Is it good?" He cuts another piece, and holds it up to

me.

I nod. “Very. Light and moist.”

His eyes darken and he shifts. “Don’t say things like that.”

“What’s wrong?” I ask, before the next forkful is placed in my open mouth. “It’s so good,” I say seductively.

He narrows his eyes, he drops the fork and stands, reaching for my hand. “Okay. Time to go now.” He reaches for his wallet and places a few bills on the table. I can’t help but giggle as I stand.

CHAPTER SIXTEEN

On the way back to Alex's I am playing my plan over in my head. I hope I don't face-plant or look like I'm having a seizure when I get my clothes off. I don't want to look like a fool. I want him to be so turned on by me. I want it to be perfect.

"Join me upstairs," I say, walking toward the stairs. I'm not asking him. I'm telling him and I think he likes it.

"Yes ma'am," he salutes me as he hurries up the stairs to catch me. Only he misses a step and trips. "Shit."

"Are you okay?" I hurry back down to him. He looks up and smiles grabbing me around the waist. He begins tickling me and I scream.

"What's this?" He can feel the strip running down my stomach.

"Don't," I say, trying to get up, swatting his hands away. "It's part of your surprise," I pout. I worked hard and have suffered all evening in this damn thing. I don't want him to spoil it now.

In the bedroom, I push him into the chair in the corner.

The look on his face shows me he's surprised, maybe intrigued, and definitely curious. I dim the lights and put on some music, turned down low. I reach into my purse, pulling the hand cuffs out and lying them on the bed. I walk back over to him and the grin on his face reminds me of a child on Christmas Eve.

"Are you going to use those on me?"

"No. But you are going to use them on me soon."

"Can we get to that part now, then?" He reaches for me, and I dodge out of his way, shaking my finger at him.

"Soon. I want to show you something first." I reach into my sweater and pull the collar out and snap it behind my neck. Alex's eyebrows go up in surprise. I slowly lift my sweater and stop for a moment, for effect, and wink at him. He has a playful glint in his eyes. The dim light's reflection make his eyes almost look like they're in flames. I slowly walk a bit closer and lower the sweater back down and decide to start with my jeans. The sweater comes to my mid-thigh and he can get the full effect of the outfit at once.

His hands clench on the arm of the chair. "You're killing me."

"That's the point. I want you to want me."

"I do want you. I want to know what's under that sweater."

I step out of my heels and slowly shimmy out of my jeans. I slip the heels back on because they complete the outfit and I know he likes them. I can now hear his shallow breathing. I know he's getting aroused with the anticipation. I haven't fallen and I'm so grateful. I look down into his hungry eyes as I slowly walk behind him and bend down, kissing his neck.

"Don't turn around."

"Okay," he whispers.

I take the sweater off and try to walk sexily back around to him. The look on his face makes it all worth it. He sucks in a deep breath. "Holy fuck, Jessa! You look so fucking sexy."

His words make me feel so good inside. I know my boobs are small and I don't have a rock-hard stomach, but his reaction makes me feel sexy. I smile shyly and whisper, "Thank you."

"Did you buy this for me?"

"I did today. I wanted to do something special for you. I can tell how hard you've been trying to overcome your issues so I planned this all out as a celebration."

"I love it. You look amazing. I'll do even better if I'll be rewarded like this."

"That can be arranged. Now what are you going to do with me?"

"I just want to look at you for a minute. Fuck! Are those crotchless panties, too? Turn around." His voice is deep, when he says it. He's so excited. It's adorable. I do a little turn for him, smiling as I'm wrapped in his arms.

"Can you wear this when you clean the house?" His

hands start roaming over my body.

"Hell no. I will not," I laugh and smack his shoulder.

He lowers me onto the bed and takes his clothes off a hell of a lot faster than I had. If I were wearing panties they'd be soaked by now. Since I'm not I can feel the wetness between my legs. I smile when he picks up the handcuffs and dangles them from his finger. I wanted this for so long. I'm excited to have my control taken away and him have all the power over me to do as he pleases. Not knowing what's going to happen has my heart racing in my chest.

Kneeling on the bed, he threads the cuffs through one bar of the headboard. He lifts one of my wrists and closes the cuff around it, then the other wrist. I pull against them gently. The fuzziness makes them not entirely uncomfortable.

"Are you okay? Are they too tight?" he asks.

"They're fine. Now what are you going to do with me?"

"How about I just show you."

Not being able to move my arms is hard. I want to touch him so badly. I want to grip his strong arms and leave scratches down his back. Instead, I grip the rails on the headboard and arch into him, thrust for thrust.

"Jessa, you look so sexy like this beneath me," he grunts, bringing his hand up to my face, caressing my cheek softly then running his fingers down the collar and the strip down my stomach. He lets my wrists go and I instantly cling to him, running my hands all over him, his chest, his forearms and his shoulders. I'm holding on for dear life as he drives inside of me. I'm close and I sense that he is, too. He has lowered himself onto his elbows and kisses me urgently. I'm gasping for breath. I feel my insides begin to spasm.

"Give it to me. Let me feel you around me, Jessa," he grunts. That's all it takes and I'm screaming his name over and over. Alex yells a guttural "Fuck" and collapses on top of me, breathing into my neck. We're both completely sated as we try to catch our breath.

Alex doesn't have to leave for Tennessee until two, so we have the day to spend together. I can't go because I need to study my notes for a test on Tuesday. Since I'm not going he wants to make the most of our day together.

He won't tell me what we're doing. He's being all secretive and cute. I hear him go out to the garage a few times, but never see what he is doing. When I asked him, and asked if he needed help he tells me no and to just relax. So, that's what I'm doing. I'm catching up on my poor neglected book. It used to take me no time to read a whole book. Now, with work, school and my awesome boyfriend, I can't find much time.

"Okay. I think I have everything ready. Do you need anything before we go?"

I laugh. "Um, if I knew what we were doing, I could

probably answer that."

"Oh. Well that is true, I guess." He briefly hesitates and looks to the ceiling. "I'm not sure what to tell you, exactly."

"How about if I need nice clothes, comfy clothes, maybe tennis shoes?"

"Yes. You need tennis shoes. You do have some here, right?" His face falls. It's like his plans may be ruined.

"I have my tennis shoes upstairs."

"Perfect. Grab them and put on those sexy yoga things you wear."

"My yoga pants and a tank?"

"Yes, those. Hurry."

"Okay. Okay. I'm going," I giggle. He is so excited. I love this side of him. The carefree man without a trouble in the world.

About an hour's drive later, we pull up at the state park. It's known for great hiking, biking, fishing, ATV trails and has a nice picnic area and gorgeous views of the countryside. I've only been here once and that was when I was a child. I'm not much of an outdoorsy girl.

"How about some outdoor time today? I love it here. I always come when I need to be alone and want to think." He looks up at the clouds.

"Sounds fun. I haven't been here since I was a little girl. My dad brought me fishing here once. Right over there," I say, pointing to the dock about hundred yards away. It makes me a little sad. I did have some nice times with my dad. I'll never understand why he left.

"We aren't fishing today. We're going to make new memories, happy ones, together." He slides across the seat, grabbing the nape of my neck, and pulls me in for a kiss on the cheek.

He slides back over quickly and hops out of the truck. I'm smiling at his child like behavior. He has come a long way in such a short time. I'm falling more in love with him each day. I didn't even think that was possible. My thoughts are interrupted as he opens my door for me. He offers me his hand to help me out. "Come on," he says, offering me his hand and helping me out. "I thought we could hike up Pinnacle Mountain and have a picnic at the top or wherever we decide to stop." He must have noticed my eyes about fall out of my head as I looked to the top of the mountain. I don't know if I could make it all the way to the top my first time but I do love a challenge.

Alex grabs a backpack out of the bed of the truck. He hands it to me and I almost drop it. It's a little heavy.

He laughs. "Sorry, wrong one," he says taking it and handing me the other backpack. I smile at him and crinkle my nose. It's not near as heavy as the one he's carrying.

"Are there rocks in yours?"

"No. It's our lunch and a few bottled waters. Yours has a blanket."

By the time we finally make it half way I'm out of breath, I'm hungry, I'm sweaty and I'm getting cranky. It's almost one and I need a break. Alex must see me struggling to keep up with him because he stops and sets his backpack down. He takes mine from me and I collapse on the hard rocks, panting.

"Are you okay? You're making that sound, the one right before I make you cum. like." If it weren't for the smile on his face right now, I'd want to throat punch him. I must say, he is in his element right now. I need to work out. Maybe I can join him at the gym sometime. I'd love to watch him lifting weights, seeing his muscles contracting. I need to think of something else, only I can't. He's taking his sweaty t-shirt off.

I groan, "Are you trying to kill me?"

"Huh?" He looks oblivious to what his body does to me.

I let out a long breath. "I can hardly breathe and you're stripping in front of me."

He looks down at his chest and smiles. "Well, do you want me to have a heat stroke?" He takes out two waters and hands me one. I watch as he opens his and pours half of it over his head and tips his head, then guzzles the rest. I watch the water roll down his body and it's so freaking sexy. I was already hot from the hike, but now I'm a totally different kind of hot.

"Damn you! Stop it!"

"What is wrong with you?" He seems confused by my actions.

"How would you like it if I took my shirt off and poured

water over my head right now?"

"I'd like it a lot, actually. Want me to help you?" He's smiling again. He kisses me and I open for him. Our tongues tie and I moan in his mouth, running my hands over his slick chest. I pull away and he looks sad. It's fake. He's even poking his lip out like a child.

"We're in public and I'm starving."

"Me, too," he says, trying to reach for me again.

"Feed me. I need food." I clarify so he doesn't try again. I feel like I could pass out at any moment. It's partly from the hike and lack of food today, but also from him. He gets me so worked up, so quickly.

Alex grabs my backpack and lays the blanket on the flattest area he can find and begins setting out our lunch. He has brought meats, cheeses, crackers and grapes and pulls out two more waters. I frown at him. He'd better not waste another bottle. Well, I guess he didn't waste the first one. It sure looked good on him.

"Earth to Jessa. Are you going to join me?"

He has it all set up for us. I shake my head and walk over sitting on the blanket. "This is really sweet of you, Alex."

"You bring it out in me. I never thought I could be this happy. There were moments I was happy with Lizzy. It was mainly in the beginning, when we first started dating. She was my first love, but that love was nothing compared to the love I feel for you. I love you so much."

"I'm so in love with you, too, Alex. I thought I was in

love with Tyler but I think it was more being comfortable. I've never felt this way, ever, with anyone. You're my first true love."

"I want to be your last." He leans in and stares into my eyes then kisses me gently.

"I want that, too. I can see myself being with you forever, Alex. You make me so happy. I was having a rough few months and you came into my life so unexpectedly at just the right time. You're my savior."

"No. I think I could say the same thing about you. I would probably be stuck at home, still stuck in my feelings, and still living in the past. I now want to look to the future and you're in it."

Those words have me in tears. I jump in his lap, causing him to laugh as he catches me. I cover his face in kisses. We're both so sweaty and still in public. Someone could come walking by at any minute and that's the only reason we are both still clothed, except for his missing shirt. I want him so badly. It's a long walk back down too. I consider it, but I know the minute we get naked we would be caught. The wait will make it so much better, but his hardness below me, pushing into my ass, is killing me. I get up and sit beside him trying to calm myself and we enjoy our picnic and the beautiful view.

CHAPTER SEVENTEEN

This day has been simply amazing. On the drive back to Alex's, all I can think about is the conversation we had during our picnic. I am so happy that Alex feels the same as I do. I have so much love for him. He's everything I've ever wanted and didn't even know it. To be loved and cherished by such a wonderful, broken man has its challenges, but I think we're getting past all of that now.

We make it back to his house with only a couple of hours before he has to leave for Tennessee I wish I could go, but I need to study. Alex understands and will be coming back tonight, since I can't. We walk into the bathroom and take our sweaty clothes off and take a shower together. He washes my hair for me and I'm in heaven. I close my eyes and lean into his chest as he massages the shampoo into my hair. He brings me under the water and rinses it out. When I open my eyes, he's looking at me with such love in his eyes. We don't speak. So much has been said today, we are just in the moment now. I put some shampoo in my hand and begin massaging it into his hair. He closes his eyes and I can see how relaxed he is. He doesn't look sad. He looks content and it's me that makes him feel this way.

After our shower, we dry off and are in our towels. Alex packs a few things he needs for work and I go downstairs for some water. I think I may be a bit dehydrated. I guzzle the bottle as Alex walks into the kitchen, still in his towel, and wraps me in his arms.

"I wish you could come with me."

"Me, too. You'll be back tonight, though. I'll make it up to you then."

"How about you start now." He lifts me and my towel falls to the floor. I wrap my legs around his waist as he carries me into the living room, his own towel falling on the way. I feel him pressing at my entrance. I want him so badly. He sets me on my feet near the couch and turns me so I'm facing away from him. He leans in and kisses the back of my neck bending me forward over the cushions. He runs his fingertips lightly down my back causing me to shiver. He steps between my legs and uses one to spread me farther for him.

"So fucking beautiful." He slowly runs a finger through my wetness causing me to gasp. "You have no idea how beautiful you are, do you?"

I don't answer him. I've never considered myself very pretty. I've always seen myself as average. I feel him press himself into my wetness the slightest bit and stop. "I love you, Jessa. I think you're beautiful inside and out. You make me a better person, the person I'm beginning to believe you deserve."

"I love you, so much. You're everything I've ever wanted. Please Alex. I want you so bad. Please." I push backwards hard and he's buried inside me. Being bent over like this has to be my new favorite position. I feel all of him so deep inside me. After a few more thrusts, I'm gone. I'm a quivering mess and Alex slows and grips my hips. He's trying to gain control, but fails as he reaches his climax and a loud moan coming from deep within. I collapse on the couch and Alex joins me with a few tissues, so I don't have any issues on his couch. Some people would hate his OCD ways, but I love them, especially since I have it, too. Maybe not as bad as him, though.

"That was so good," I pant.

"You're so good," he says, kissing my forehead. As good as it was, something feels off suddenly. I'm not sure what it is. I guess knowing Alex will be leaving very soon has me a bit off, but something doesn't seem right.

"What's wrong?"

"I'm not sure. I just have a weird feeling is all."

"Well that's not good after what amazing feelings we just shared."

"I know. Maybe it's just knowing you're leaving me," I pout, snuggling into his side.

"I'll be back tonight. Maybe about ten or eleven. I need to just look over the job and sign a few papers and I'll hurry back here, to you."

"You want me to stay while you're gone?"

"Yes. If you want to?"

"Okay. Sure," I smile.

Alex gets dressed and then grabs his briefcase as we walk to the door to the garage. He looks so good in his button up and jeans. His arms fill out every shirt he owns. I'm still not used to so much muscle.

Alex skims his finger down the buttons of the shirt of his I'm wearing. "I like you in my shirts," he says.

"I like wearing them. They're the perfect night shirts for me."

"I like you in nothing," he says, leaning in for a kiss before he leaves. It crosses my mind to say fuck it and go with him, but I do need to study. This will give me alone time to concentrate and have no distractions.

"I love you and I'll text you on my way home. There's some food in the fridge, if you get hungry."

"I love you, too." He kisses me once more before walking out the door. That weird feeling still lingering. I'm sure everything will be fine.

I watch him drive away from the living room window. After he's out of sight I sigh and look around the quiet house. It still feels weird to be here without him, but I am comfortable being here alone. I grab my notes from my backpack and sit on the couch with a blanket. It smells like him. That then makes me think of what we just did on this couch, his loving words and how he knows my body better than I do. My mind is wondering when I should be studying. Maybe I need a snack. I go to the fridge and get the leftover grapes from our picnic and sit back down. I read my notes for a couple of hours and am already sick of it. I should have gone with him. I could have read the notes on the way there and while he was working. What was I thinking, damn it?

I walk to the window and look out at the beautiful flowers just past the porch. There are a few beautiful butterflies flying around them. Even seeing all the beauty around me I can't shake the eerie feeling I have in the pit of my stomach. I decide to text Brittany. She should be off work in about an hour. Maybe we could go have dinner and I can shake this feeling.

Hey bitch! Are you almost off work?

I am hoe. What are you doing? You'd better not say my uncle either.

Nah that was hours ago. He had to run to Tennessee to check that job.

Oh, yeah. I forgot. I've been swamped today.

I wanted to see if you wanted to get dinner. I'm sick of studying?

Ok. Yeah, I can do that. I should be finished here in about thirty minutes. Where are you?

Thanks! I'm at Alex's.

Alone?

Lol! Yeah why?

Wow Jessa he must trust you. You are so good for him. Again, you're welcome lol!

Thanks! We're getting pretty serious lately.

I'll come there and we can decide from there.

Ok. See ya soon.

I walk upstairs and change into the only other clothes I brought with me. I honestly had no idea what Alex's plans were so I packed a skirt and a matching tank. I also have a light jacket to wear over it. I throw my hair in a bun. I don't have much time left so I put on mascara and some lip gloss.

On my way back downstairs, the doorbell rings. Brittany's right on time. I open the door and she hurries inside.

"Remember that car that kept driving past the office the

other day?"

I freeze. "Yes. Why?"

"I saw it again today. A couple of times passing by the office and then when I was coming here I saw it leaving this very road." I feel all the color drain from my face.

"Jessa, do you know who that is? You look like you've seen a ghost. Are you okay?"

"I'm fine. If you promise not to say anything to Alex, I'll tell you okay?"

"Are you cheating on him?" She looks angry.

"Are you fucking kidding right now? You know me better than that! It's Tyler."

"Your ex?" She looks confused.

"Yes. He seems to have a problem with me being with your uncle and I believe he's now stalking me. I saw him that day at the office, I just didn't say anything. I also ran into him yesterday while I was at a boutique." She doesn't need to know which one. She'd probably puke.

"Do you feel unsafe? You can always call the police, you know?"

"I think he'll get over it soon enough. We were together for so long. I think it's just hard for him to see that I've moved on."

"That fucker cheated on you. Why the hell is he acting like a crazy person? He'd better hope I don't see him again near the office. I'm fucking serious. I'll call the police." I smile because I know she will.

"If he continues it I will I promise. Please don't tell Alex. He's come so far. I'm afraid he'll go all cave man. I don't want him to have a setback."

"He has Jessa. All because of you, he's doing so good now. I haven't seen him in the office in over a year and when he came in earlier this week, I thought I would die. I've very much enjoyed him helping in the office, but I still need more help. I kinda left early, so you can't mention me being here this early, okay?"

"Your secret's safe with me," I laugh. "Seriously, though, if this gets any worse with Tyler, I will call the police and I'll also tell Alex. I promise."

"So, do you think we should go out knowing he's lurking around?" She seems a little scared.

"Yes. I don't think he'd do anything. I'm not going to live in fear of him, either. You remember what a pussy he was in school. I don't think we need to worry, but if he's still out he will be looking for my car. Could we take yours?"

"Yeah. Sure."

Soon after our conversation we arrive at the best Mexican restaurant in town. It's busy on Friday nights but luckily we are seated at a two-person booth. I'm so glad. I hate tables and so does Brittany. Another one of the random things we have in common.

A waiter brings us chips and salsa along with our menus.

"May I have a margarita with sugar, please?" I ask.

"Make that two but with salt for me, please," she smiles.

"Sure," he says with his Spanish accent.

I eat a few chips, before speaking. "So, we haven't gotten a chance to catch up lately. Guess who's in one of my classes?"

"I don't know who?"

"Fucking Tyler. I think it's kind of how it all began."

"Can you transfer into another class?"

"It was the only one left. The rest are full. Remember Julie from school?"

"The nerdy one?"

I frown, "Well, yeah, but she's really nice. She's in my classes with me. I was thinking maybe we could take her out one night when we do a girl's night?"

"Sure, I guess we could. Does she still dress the same?"

I laugh. "Don't be a bitch, but yes she does."

The waiter arrives with our drinks and more chips. We've already finished the first basket. I'm glad because now the tequila has something to settle on.

"Have you decided what you'd like to order?" he asks.

I wasn't sure if I wanted the chimichanga or the quesadilla. "I'll have the chimichanga please."

"I'll have the grilled chicken quesadilla please," Brittany says, closing her menu.

"Good choices. I'll get that right in for you," the waiter smiles and takes our menus before walking away.

Our food comes before we've even finished our drinks. The service here is great and the food is always delicious. We gossip a bit on celebrity news that I'm obviously not getting to hear much of lately. We enjoy our food and finish our drinks, waiting for the bill to come. It's now even more busy than before and our poor waiter is running around like a chicken with his head cut off.

"Ladies, so sorry about your wait," he says while another table is trying to get his attention. "Here are your checks. I'll be back in just a minute," he sighs, looking at the rude people at the next table over.

We ended up leaving enough cash to cover our bills and a nice tip for him. He was a great waiter. He'd just gotten busy is all. No need for us to be rude. We reach Brittany's car and I have that weird feeling again. I look around for Tyler's car, but I don't see it.

"What's wrong, Jessa?" Brittany asks before getting in.

"I don't know. I have a weird feeling again. I've been having it since Alex left this afternoon," I tell her, shaking my head and then getting in the car.

"Do you think it's because of Tyler?"

"I'm starting to think so," I say, looking around. I still see no sign of his car anywhere. "Maybe I'm just being paranoid. I don't know."

"Well, you're starting to freak me out about it," she says. "Do you want to come to my house until Alex gets back tonight?"

"No. I'm not letting Tyler get to me. He's probably just trying to scare me. He wants me to take him back and I flat out told him no."

Brittany smirks. "If he wants you back, he's going about it all wrong."

"I hope he's given up by now. I'm happy and it makes me realize how unhappy I was with Tyler. I don't know why I stayed as long as I did. He was just familiar, I guess."

"I don't know, either. I saw back then what a dick head he was. I always wondered what you saw in him. I thought maybe he had a big dick or something. Maybe he had a wicked tongue."

I crack up laughing, "No, he doesn't have either. He never wanted to go down on me. He was so strange. Now Alex..."

"Shut the fuck up right now. I don't need to hear any of this. It's fucking gross." I can understand why she wouldn't want to hear about her uncle and our sex life, but it's still funny as hell to get her all flustered.

"I know. I know. I was just joking."

"That's not a joke, Jessa. That could give me nightmares," she shivers and I die laughing. Those margaritas were stout tonight and I'm having too much fun with her. I'm glad, too. It keeps my mind off Tyler and his craziness.

"Let me know if you need anything," Brittany says dropping me back off at Alex's.

"I will. I promise," I tell her, looking around.

"Are you sure you don't want me to stay until Alex gets back?"

"I'll be fine."

"Alex has a pistol in his bedside table for protection against intruders." My face is utter shock. I hadn't thought of Tyler being physical to that extent, but I didn't think he'd bruise my arm, either.

"Just in case," she says.

I shrug it off. That's just silly. "I'll be fine. Now go home bitch."

"Okay. I'm not far if you need me."

"Thank you," I say and she pulls away and I hurry inside and lock the door.

CHAPTER EIGHTEEN

I study for a couple of hours and doze off on the couch. I wake up hearing someone at the door. Alex must not have his house key. I hurry to the front, all excited to see him and open the door. I try my best to shut it just as quickly, but I can't. He's stronger than me. It's Tyler and he looks crazed. I don't know what's wrong with him. I scream and try to overpower him, but I can't. He bursts through the door and I fly backwards into the wall. I'm dazed as I try to get up, and fall backwards. He's standing above me, looking down at me like he wants to kill me. I feel helpless, but I'm not that helpless girl. I move as fast as I can and kick upwards connecting with his tiny balls. He yelps and drops to his knees, holding himself with two hands, when one would obviously work just fine. I get up quickly, hurrying for the stairs.

"You fucking bitch. You're gonna pay for that you fucking whore," he yells running after me. I run faster, still a bit dizzy and slam the master bedroom door behind me. I rush to Alex's side of the bed and search for his gun in the drawer. Just as I get it in my hand, Tyler flies through the door. I jump, and quickly point it at him. He stops in his tracks. I find the safety button and switch it off.

He laughs, standing in the doorway. “What are you gonna do with that? Are you gonna shoot me?” The look in his eyes is something I’ve never seen before. I’m not sure if he’s lost his mind or if he’s on something.

My hands are shaking as I hold a gun for the first time in my life. I’ve seen enough movies to know what to do but I hope it doesn’t come to that. I don’t’ want to shoot him. “I will if you come any closer. What the fuck is wrong with you?”

“I want you back, Jessa. How fucking clear do I have to be? You’re mine,” he roars between his teeth.

“You’re crazy. You don’t own me. You fucked my best friend remember? What makes you think I’d ever take you back?” I know I should be calm. I don’t need to piss him off more, but I have the gun and thanks to the fear mixed with adrenaline, I don’t fucking care.

Tyler laughs like a psychopath. “If you want it rough Jessa, I can give it to you rough. Why don’t you wear that slutty outfit and go downstairs and bend over his couch? My face goes pale at hearing those words.

“You watched us? You sick fuck. What’s happened to you? Why would you do that?” I don’t understand what’s happened to him these last few months. He never got this angry when we were together, ever.

“I’ve been following you for a while now. I wanted to

see what was so great about the asshole you've been seeing." He pauses, and looks around the room, letting out a low whistle. "I guess you've moved up, haven't you?"

"It has nothing to do with his money. He's a good man and makes me happier than I've ever been."

Tyler tsks as he shakes his head. "No. He just likes having you as his maid and he gets to fuck you, too. It's a win-win, Jessa. He's using you. Don't you see that? Or are you too fucking blind?"

He takes a step forward, as I step back. "You have no idea what you're talking about. You know nothing about our relationship. We love each other. I love him more than I ever loved you." He makes a quick move forward and I scream and raise the gun up, meeting his face, stopping him from coming any closer."

"You won't shoot me." He laughs again. A creak in the floor has us both looking to the door. Alex is standing in the doorway with his fists balled ready to kill Tyler; his chest heaving. He barrels into Tyler, tackling him to the floor. I start crying, so happy that he's come home early.

"What the fuck is going on here? Why are you in my house? Did you fucking hurt her?" He screams in Tyler's face. I reach for my phone, which had fallen on the floor when I was looking for the gun. I dial 9-1-1; the woman on the other end says an officer is on the way.

"They're on the way." I say, still shaking with the gun in my hand.

"Jessa are you okay?" he asks, still holding Tyler down.

"I'm fine. I'm so glad you're here," I say, still crying.

"Get the fuck off me," Tyler says, trying to break free. Alex punches him in the face causing, blood to fly and the cracking sound of, Tyler's nose breaking. I hear the sirens and realize I'm still holding the gun. I turn the safety on, drop it on the bed, and collapse to the floor in tears as the officer comes in the door with his gun pointing down at Alex and Tyler as he surveys the scene.

"Ma'am, are you okay?"

Alex gets up, letting go of Tyler, "I want to press charges on this piece of shit. He tried to attack my girlfriend."

"I'm Trooper Ellis. Ma'am can you please tell me exactly what happened?"

"Yes, sir. He barged in the house and tried to attack me. I hurried upstairs for the gun to protect myself," I say, nodding to the gun on the bed.

"I'll get statements from the both of you shortly. Get up," he says to Tyler, putting him in cuffs and reading him his rights, walking him down to his police car.

Alex rushes over to me. "Jessa are you sure you're okay?" He's searching me over to make sure. I nod and he wraps me in his arms.

"I'm okay. I hit my head on the wall when he forced himself through the door, but I'm fine." Feeling Alex's arms around me, I feel safe again. I'm so glad he came when he did. I'm not sure what would have happened.

"I'm here. I'm never leaving you again," he says, kissing my forehead. "How did you know I had a gun?"

"Please don't be mad, okay? Tyler had been following me. I finally told Brittany this evening. She's noticed his car a few times and I couldn't keep it from her any longer. After she and I had dinner, she told me you had one and where it was just in case. I'm sorry I didn't tell you."

"Why didn't you tell me?" He doesn't sound happy. He's not mad, but maybe disappointed.

"I didn't think he'd do anything and I didn't want you to worry."

"Well, when I called and you didn't answer I was worried. When I pulled into the driveway and the front door was wide open, I was fucking terrified. I thought I'd lost you." I can feel him trembling. "Then I heard Tyler yelling at you and I hurried upstairs.

I pull away and look up at him. "I'm so sorry I kept it from you. I'll never keep anything from you again. I promise." I'm in tears again and Alex grips my waist tighter. We hold each other a few more minutes and then walk downstairs to give our statements.

We each write down our version of the events. Officer Ellis assures us Tyler won't be bothering us again. He found cocaine in Tyler's pocket. He's never done drugs that I know of. I look in the police car and see Tyler staring at us. He still seems to be so angry. I'm not sure if he would have hurt me, or if he would've tried to kill me, because he couldn't have me back. I don't want to know. I'm just glad Alex got home when he did. He saved me.

"There will be a court date that you both will need to attend to be sure justice is served," Trooper Ellis say giving us each a card before leaving with Tyler in the back.

Things go back to normal over the next couple of months. Tyler is still in jail and I was told he will be going to a year-long drug rehabilitation center for his heroine addiction. It was revealed in the court hearing that he's been doing heroine for years. It kind of explains some of his behavior while we were together. It makes me sometimes wonder if things could have been different for us. I can't help it and it seems terrible, but I'm so glad we didn't work out.

I finish up my business classes and end with a 3.9 GPA, which is pretty great. I've been working my ass off. It helps so much, keeping my mind off Tyler and what happened. Alex and Brittany are taking me out to celebrate and have some sort of news, something they want to talk to me about.

We're meeting at a new restaurant in town. I've heard great things about the food and am excited, and starving. I've been putting applications in around town today. I applied for a couple of receptionist jobs and an assistant position at my mom's law firm. I doubt I'll get it, even though I'm related to one of the lawyers. But, had to try. My mom is extremely proud of me.

Alex has gotten her renovations done and she's over the

moon impressed at the work and how quickly it was done. She seems to love Alex now. I knew she would, eventually. I, on the other hand, wasn't too excited because the house now has a 'for sale' sign out front and my time is limited to find another place to live before it sells. Brittany has offered me her spare bedroom, but I don't know if I should even though it would be awesome to live with my favorite bitch.

I pull in to the Italian restaurant and see Alex and Brittany talking beside his truck. They see me pull in and smile at me.

"Hey bitch," she says as I get out of my car.

"Hey whore," I smile.

Alex is shaking his head and laughing at us, "Hey babe, how was the job hunt?"

"It went well. I hope to hear back soon." I kiss him passionately as Brittany makes gagging sounds. I laugh as I pull away. Alex takes my hand in his and we all walk into the restaurant.

It's not too fancy, but has a cute look to it. There are checkered-clothed tables with chef décor on the walls. It smells delicious causing my stomach to growl.

Alex looks at me funny and then smiles, "Hungry?"

"Yes. I'm starved," I say, licking my lips. He lifts a brow and I wink at him.

We find a booth and that makes me very happy. We decide on an order of mozzarella sticks and a couple of pizzas. I love mushrooms and Brittany likes them, too. Alex hates them so he orders a meat lovers all for himself.

"So, what did you want to talk to me about?" They look at each other, and Alex clears his throat. Shit. He's nervous about what he wants to say. Now I'm nervous.

"Well, I wanted to see if you'd consider working for me, with Brittany, in the office. She needs help." I don't know what to say.

"Why the hell did I put all those applications in today if you wanted me to work for you?"

"I didn't know, until you told me this morning about that and Brittany and I had this planned for this evening," he smiles, trying to ease my annoyance.

"That sounds great. I'd love to."

"Yay! I can't wait to have you there with me," Brittany dances in her chair. "Now ask her the other thing, Alex." I stare at them both confused.

He clears his throat again. "I... well, I know you need a place to stay soon. We've been together a while now and I love you. I want you to move in with me. What do you think?"

Brittany squeals, "Say yes, Jessa!"

"Shut up," Alex says shaking his head and I laugh at him. He is so nervous waiting for my answer.

"Yes," I smile. "I would love to live with you."

"Really? You will?" He pulls me in and hugs me. I think we both forget we're in a restaurant surrounded by a bunch of other diners.

"Okay y'all. You're gonna cause us to get kicked out,"

Brittany whispers.

I giggle, pulling away and looking around, noticing a few people watching us. I don't like attention drawn to me.

"When can you move in?" Alex's excitement is contagious.

"Well, I don't have much at mom's, but I did tell her I'd help her pack up the house."

"I'll hire a moving company. Neither of you will have to pack a thing."

"I can't ask you to do that, Alex."

"You didn't. I offered." Before I could protest, he gives me a quick kiss on the cheek.

"Okay. I guess that would be a big help. I'll talk with mom to make sure she's okay with it."

"She is. I already asked her."

I frown. "You were so sure I'd say yes, weren't you?"

"Well, I was hopeful. I wanted to have all my bases covered if you did say yes, and you did, so I have everything taken care of." I shake my head and laugh.

"I'm so happy for y'all. I can't wait for us to be working together. Oh, and no sex stuff in the office. That's a deal breaker for me," Brittany says, reaching for another mozzarella stick.

Alex and I look to each other, and he gives me a wink. "Too late," I die laughing.

"Y'all are fucking gross. I knew it."

Our pizzas arrive and we enjoy our dinner. We talk

about what the job entails and what I'll be expected to do and all that jazz. I'm so lucky to have them in my life. I can't wait to start this job. I'm going to kick ass at it. I'm happy to take some of the stress off Brittany. She works so hard. That disaster of a desk shows that. And I'll soon be living with Alex. It will be my home, too. I can't wait to wake up with him every morning and going to bed with him every night.

CHAPTER NINETEEN

Alex wastes no time getting the movers scheduled. A week later, the house is completely packed and everything's loaded. Mom and I take a moment to look around the empty house.

She pulls me closer to her. "Honey, I'm so proud of you and so happy that you've found such an amazing man to spend your life with. I can hear wedding bells for you soon."

I roll my eyes. "Mom. Don't. I'm happy just the way things are right now."

"I know you are, sweetie," she gives me a kiss on my cheek before taking a final look around.

"Well, I think that's everything. I checked every drawer and closet upstairs. It's empty."

"It looks weird, doesn't it? I loved this house. Now a new family can make memories here." She starts to tear up and I hug her.

"Whoever buys it will love it as much as we did, mom."

"Okay. You still have your key to check in until it sells?"

"Yes, mom. I'll drop in to check on it."

"Thank you. I guess that's it then. Let's get home to our

men." She glances back, with a lingering tear, as we walk out and she locks the door.

"I love you mom. I'll see you soon." I hug her once more.

"I love you, too, baby girl."

I pull into the driveway of my new home. My home with Alex. I'm loving the sound of it. He comes out onto the porch with a smile on his face as I walk up.

"Welcome home," he says with an infectious smile.

I run out of the car, and jump into his arms. "Thank you. I'm so excited to get to wake up with you every morning."

He moans, "Me, too. I had the movers bring all your boxes upstairs. I've already hung up your clothes. I also took Lizzy's stuff out of the drawers and packed them in boxes. I wasn't sure of the order you like your socks and panties so I left that for you."

"Thank you, Alex. I'm so proud of you. I know that couldn't have been easy for you."

"It wasn't as bad as I'd thought it would be. I needed to do it a long time ago. You helped me realize that." He hugs me tighter. "I did find something that kind of shocked me a bit." He gives me a pointed look.

"What?" I'm not sure what could be so shocking.

"Well, come inside and I'll show you," he smirks.

I follow him inside and he's acting like the cat that's

gotten the canary. He turns around facing me and pulls out Bob. Oh my God! I'd forgotten all about him. I haven't needed him in a long time. I feel my face heating. I don't know what to say. I want to slap him right now. He's grinning so big.

"Impressive," he says, wiggling him around in his hand.

"Stop that. You might drop him!" I reach for it, but Alex lifts it above his head.

"Him. It's a him? You sound like it's a person or something." He scrunches up his face, trying to act pissed.

"That is Bob and he was my savior before you came along," I say, reaching for it again.

He's rolling with laughter, now. "Bob. You named it Bob?"

"Of course I named him. I loved him for a while," I smile, trying to play along, even though I'm truly mortified. I should have put him in my purse when I was packing. I had no idea Alex would unpack my stuff.

"Tonight, I think I'll have to see how good Bob pleases you," his eyes smolder, as he steps closer to me.

"You mean you want to use him on me? You're not mad?"

"What? Why would I be mad? I think it's hot. I want to taste you while I play with it inside of you."

"I don't know. I always had to hide him. I knew if Tyler found him he would've been pissed and thrown it away. He would've said I was cheating with a vibrator or something."

"Jessa, you know he had, and still has issues. It's not a big deal to me at all. I think it could be a lot of fun." He wiggles his eyebrows before glancing back at Bob.

I notice some of my pictures around the living room and it warms my heart that he's making me feel so welcome. It's his home, but now it's mine, too. I can't believe I live in this beautiful house. There's not anything I'd want to change, either. I love everything about it.

Walking into the kitchen I notice my magnets on the fridge. I'm shocked he's okay that my book swag, with bare chested men on them, are on his fridge. He could be on a book cover. I turn around and smile, "Thanks for putting the magnets up. I wasn't allowed to have them on the fridge in the apartment."

"I'm not intimidated one bit."

"You could be on one, ya know?"

"You think so? I don't know." He shakes his head.

"Are you serious? Look at these arms," I squeeze them. "Look at this chest," lifting his shirt up, running my hands across the ridges of his six pack. "And these pecs," tweaking his nipples. He's watching my hands as they move across his soft skin and his mouth is open a little and I feel his breath on my forehead. His heart is also racing. I'm turning him on, touching him and talking about his body. I never imagined I could do this to someone like him. Someone so hot. I don't think he even knows how hot he is.

"If you keep touching me like this, I'm gonna have to

take you upstairs to our bed."

"I love hearing that. Our bed." I wrap my arms around his waist. "Can Bob join us?"

"Uh, can you please never say that again. It sounds like another man is joining us. I will never share you." The look on his face is priceless. He looks horrified and it makes me bust out laughing.

"I wanted to make you supper for your first night in your new home. What would you like to have?"

"That's sweet, but I was hoping for some takeout so we can go to bed."

"Are you tired?"

I smile, "No, not tired at all."

I finally see he gets it. "How about Chinese?"

"That sounds perfect."

After supper, we hurry up the stairs to bed. He takes off his shirt and jumps into bed and I join him. I snuggle into his strong arms and sigh. I see more of my pictures on the dresser and my side table. Some of me and my mom and a couple of my dad. I don't know why I still have them. There's also a new picture on his side. It's a picture of me.

"When did you take that?"

"When you were sleeping."

"I can see that," I laugh.

"Do you like it? I thought you looked so beautiful, so peaceful and the sunrise coming in around your beautiful face. I had to take it."

"I wish I saw myself as you do," I say, kissing his chest.

"Jessa, you are a beautiful woman. Inside and out. I love everything about you. I even love your snoring." He starts digging into my ribs causing me to squirm and giggle.

"I do not snore!" I move away from him as if I'm pouting.

"Oh yes you do," he laughs. "I'll record you next time."

"Whatever. You still love me, though."

"I sure do. Now get over here." He pulls me on top of him. "Let's get these clothes off." Before I can start, he's already lifting my shirt over my head and removing my bra. He leans up and kisses each nipple then draws one into his mouth. I arch into his mouth and bring my fingers into his hair.

"Raise up," he says softly, dragging my pants down my thighs and I wiggle out of them. "I want to taste you. Scoot up here and sit on my chest. You can rest your hands on the headboard." I've never done this before. So many firsts with Alex. I do as he says and try not to put all my weight on him. I look down on him and he smiles a devilish smile and licks his lips. I swear it's the hottest thing I've ever seen.

One swipe of his tongue across my clit, eyes still on mine and I can't possibly look away. This is so erotic seeing him lick me in this position.

"You taste so good Jessa, so addicting," he says before sucking my clit into his mouth.

I groan, "You're so good at it, too." He reaches under

the pillow and pulls out Bob and smiles.

"How do I turn it on," he turns it over, looking for a switch I guess.

"You twist the bottom." I can't believe he's about to use my vibrator on me.

Alex turns it on and the vibration begins in his hand, along with the loud buzzing sound. "Wow," he says, his eyebrows raising. "Powerful," he says and I giggle.

Alex licks and sucks a bit more before positioning Bob at my entrance, circling. "Raise up on your knees." I do and he drags Bob through my wetness up to my throbbing clit and I moan, gripping the headboard. He brings it back down and pushes inside and clamping his mouth over my clit at the same time. He sucks and flicks his tongue at the same time as he pumps Bob, I mean the vibrator, inside of me. It feels so fucking good. I feel myself getting close already. I can hear how wet I am each time he moves it in and out. He's licking my clit and goes down lapping up my juices and moans. "Fuck! You're so wet, Jessa."

I bring one hand behind me and stroke his erection through his jeans. I try to unbutton them but with what he's doing to me it's too hard so I give up and grip the headboard again. I feel my orgasm building quickly. My breathing quickens. He knows I'm close and pumps faster and puts more pressure on my clit as he licks harder and faster, moving his face side to side quickly. My head falls back and the ecstasy floods me. I scream with the intensity of his tongue and the vibrator. The convulsions seem to last forever. Alex pulls the vibrator out, turning it off and continues licking me softly, riding out my pleasure until I collapse on his face.

"Oh. My. God. Alex that was amazing." I hear mumbles. "I'm so sorry," raising up off his face.

"It was so good you thought you'd smother me," he laughs.

I smile, "Now it's your turn," I say, kissing down his chest. I unbutton his pants and pull them down to his thighs. I grab Bob and his face scrunches up. He starts to say something and I shake my head. I've read that a vibrator on a man's balls while giving head is very pleasurable. I want to try it and I think Alex might be surprised. I hope he likes it.

Turning it on, I wrap one hand around the base of his erection and drag the head across my lips. Alex's eyes are glazed over with need, watching my movements. I think he's curious about how I'm going to use the vibrator on him. He could be worried, too. I smile at the thought. I lick the tip and bring him inside, all the way back, his happy trail tickling my nose and I moan deeply causing him to suck in a deep breath through his teeth, his head falling back onto the headboard. I start sucking slowly, torturing him with each flick of my tongue on the tip. I use my other hand and bring the vibrator up to his balls as I go down and back up.

"Oh fuck, Jessa!" he cries, lifting his head. His fingers slide into my hair. His legs begin to tremble. I palm his balls and add more pressure with the vibrator. I circle the head and clamp around his length and suck faster. I taste a bit of his saltiness. I know he's close. I bring him all the way in and swallow. He's groaning and fisting my hair but never loses control. I suck the head hard and pump him with my hand. I feel him tense, "I'm close, Jessa. Fuck! So good," he moans. I feel the hot liquid hit the back of my throat and I swallow quickly, sucking every last drop.

I lay beside him and snuggle into his side. I think he enjoyed that very much; it didn't take as long for him to get his.

"So, how did you like that?"

"I don't wanna admit it, but I liked it. How did you know to do that?"

"I read it in a book," I laugh.

"Hhhhmmmm." That's all he says and then kisses my forehead. "I love you." He pulls me closer to him.

"I love you, too."

It's been a wonderful welcome to my new home. My new life with Alex. We drift off to sleep together in *our* bed.

CHAPTER TWENTY

Monday rolls around and Alex and I ride in to the office together. I'm so excited to start my new job. I feel pretty in my slacks and blouse that Alex helped me pick out and I'm confident I can do a great job. Brittany is ecstatic, too. I'll be taking a lot of stress off her and it should be fun working together.

We arrive a little early so I can get my desk set up and the laptop up and running. Alex also wants to go over a few things that I'll be doing. It's nothing too hard. I'll answer phones, keep track of logs on the company vehicles, payroll, and other things.

Alex goes into his office to start his day and I'm sitting at my desk. I didn't notice how nice it is the last time I was here. I was too concerned about Tyler stalking me and then preoccupied in Alex's office. Oh, let's not forget Brittany's disaster of a desk. Looking at it now I notice she's kept it clean and organized. With me here it should be able to stay that way.

I take a moment, to look at my surroundings. On one wall, there are a couple of photos hanging. I walk over to look at them. I see a younger Alex, not nearly as built as he is now. I take a closer look. Damn, he was hot back then. Standing next to him is who must be his father. Alex looks a lot like him, same facial structure and hair color. His mother is on the other side and she seems very happy with a big smile on her face. Alex has her smile. They look like a great family.

I walk back to my desk as Brittany comes in.

"Hey bitch," she says. "You look hot!"

"Thanks skank!"

"So, how's it going?"

"Slow. No one's called or come in yet."

"Yeah. It will pick up soon. The crew and salesmen will be coming in any minute now." She rolls her eyes.

"What's that about?"

"You'll see."

A few minutes later the crews start to roll in and out. One salesman comes in and he's cute.

"Who are you?"

"I'm Jessa. I'm helping Brittany in the office."

He nods, "I'm George. I'm glad you're here to help. She needs it." He laughs at his own joke, as he goes to grab file from a cabinet.

I turn to Brittany as soon as he's gone. "He's cute!"

She nods. "Yes, and very married with a handful of kids."

A few minutes later a tall man in a polo shirt comes walking in. He has tattoos all over his arms. He's fucking hot.

Dark brown hair and dark eyes. I look to Brittany and she has her face stuck in her phone oblivious to who's walked in.

"You're new," he says.

Brittany barely looks at him, before going back to her phone. "You're observant."

"Hi. I'm Jessa. I'm working in the office with Brittany." I smile and look away. His eyes are gorgeous. I wonder what his story is.

"I'm Nathan. I'm one of the salesman. The best one," he smiles, displaying his beautiful white teeth. He walks over to Brittany and sits on the edge of her desk.

"Get off my fucking desk!" She makes a show of pushing him away. "How many times do I have to tell you that?"

"Every time," he winks at her. "I like getting you wound up."

"Why do you have to drive me crazy? It doesn't help you at all. You know that right?"

Poor Nathan's smile fades. "Well, since Jessa's working here maybe you'll have time to go out with me now?"

"Just stop, Nathan," Brittany says irritated getting back to work on her laptop. I wonder what the problem is with them? He's super hot and seems to be nice. Maybe a bit annoying but still not a deal breaker for a date with her. He gets up from her desk and walks towards the door. Turning back to us, he says, "Have a great day ladies."

I smile, "You, too." He smiles and looks towards Brittany before walking out the door.

"What the hell, Brittany?"

She looks up from her laptop, "What?" She doesn't follow what I'm pertaining too.

"Why are you so bitchy towards him?"

"Nathan? He gets on my fucking nerves. He doesn't give up."

"Why aren't you interested in him? He's fucking hot."

"His divorce was just finalized a few weeks ago. I know because he made it a point to tell me. His ex-wife is a psycho. She'd call all the time making sure he was working and she'd call to see what time he'd left each day, too. She didn't trust him at all. They have a two-year-old son together. I'm not wanting to be involved in all that drama. He is hot, though, isn't he?"

"Who's hot?" Alex says coming from his office. He walks over to my desk and kisses me.

"Okay, y'all. This is a work environment and I'm not dealing with all this PDA. Take it to your office. Scratch that don't do that either, gross." She shudders looking at her uncle. She then smiles at him and he rolls his eyes. She likes to bust his balls every chance she gets. I think it's hilarious.

"Nathan has a thing for Brittany and she's such a bitch to him." I give her an evil eye and she scowls.

"Brittany, he's a really nice guy. Don't hold his crazy ex-wife against him. He is a great asset to this company."

"This is not gang up on Brittany day. I don't need y'all playing matchmaker. Got it?" She gives us both a pointed look before going back to her computer.

"Okay," we both say in unison, laughing at each other. Brittany smiles and shakes her head at us.

The day goes on and I answer the phone a few times. Nothing too major has happened today. Brittany said it's been a slow day. A few of the crew members come in and a foreman, putting in supply orders for a job they're working on. They all seemed to be nice enough. It's been a great first day.

CHAPTER TWENTY-ONE

A month later…

I'm feeling great about my new job. I'm learning a lot about Alex's company. I've thought of a few ways to make things easier and more organized for him and he loves my ideas.

Alex, Brittany, and I have lunch together each day. Some days we're so busy we don't get a chance to leave, but manage to get a quick bite in the breakroom. I've gotten to know the other employees, too. Alex has a great group of people working for him and I'm grateful to be one of them. They all know that Alex and I are together, and none of them treat me any differently because of it and I'm glad. I want to be taken serious. I believe I'm a good worker and want to be respected.

—

As the weeks go by, I'm more comfortable in Alex's home, *our* home. I am still not used to saying that. He makes me feel as if it's every bit my own. Alex even allows me into the library where all Lizzy's books are neatly organized on the many shelves. He offered to box them up and I flat out refused. I've added the few I have on the bottom of one shelf. I love it. The smell of books and the beautiful wood and comfortable seating. I find myself in the library a lot, reading and relaxing, if not on the patio, surrounded by the beautiful flowers in bloom. I've even gotten him to allow me to read some to him. We always end up in the bedroom afterwards.

He's come such a long way in a short time. He's now the man I had always seen inside that I knew he could be. He's happy and we're so in love. We're doing so well together. I love him more every day, if that's even possible.

I never thought I'd have a job I love, Brittany becoming my best friend, a boyfriend I love and adore, and to be living in this amazing house that we share together. If it weren't for Brittany, I don't think I would have met Alex. If it weren't for Tyler being such a fuck up, I probably wouldn't have ever reconnected with Brittany. I would have had no reason to be putting up those flyers that day. She's been a great friend. I hope, now that I'm working with her, she can find more time for herself and find a great guy. I think Nathan could be him, but she's not so sure. Maybe that will change. I hope it does.

Now knowing the issues Tyler has, I'm not sure he would've ever changed. I think things would have only gotten worse with his addiction. I can't believe I never knew what all he was hiding from me, the drugs, women and God only knows what else.

Things might have been different between us if he would have confided in me and wanted help. I sometimes still think about that night in Alex's bedroom. If I hadn't grabbed that gun, what would he have done? I only hope that he's getting the help he needs.

He wrote me a letter, apologizing about everything he'd put me through and hoping that Alex makes me truly happy. I feel that gives me the closure I need to finally put it all in the past. I didn't reply. I'm sure he understands why. I just want to forget and move on. I have a wonderful life now with amazing people in it. I couldn't ask for anything better.

Well, maybe one thing could make it better, a puppy. I want one so bad. I can't decide whether I want a small dog or a big dog. You can't do too much with the small ones. I mean they'll play fetch and all, but I don't want to have to worry about stepping on the damn thing all the time. I think Weimaraners are beautiful and they don't shed. At least I don't think so. I need to read into that. I think I almost have Mr. OCD talked into it, though.

EPILOGUE

SIX MONTHS LATER...

Ben is five months old now and finally house-trained. I won Alex over on getting a puppy and we decided on a yellow lab. I was kind of shocked and didn't know they shed so much, but they're wonderful family dogs. His hair isn't as bad as say the brown or black labs so I'm hoping Alex doesn't have a heart attack with all the hair everywhere as he gets bigger. I do sweep a lot, that's for sure.

Alex invited my mom, her now husband Edward, Brittany, his parents, and everyone from the company over for a BBQ today. We've been working so much, we haven't had much time for any family time, or fun for that matter. Alex thought it would be a great way to thank the employees for their hard work and see family as well.

I'm working on the side dishes in the house while Alex mans the grill outside. We have quite a few people coming so there's a massive amount of food to prepare. Mom, Alex's mom Martha, and Brittany are helping me while the men are gathered around the grill with Alex having a few beers. His mom is very sweet; her and my mom are chatting it up. We're making potato salad, baked beans, macaroni salad, stuffed mushrooms and asparagus. I made a cake and cookies for dessert last night. Alex helped me with those and even wore one of my flowery aprons. He had nothing on underneath. I'll say it was the fastest I'd ever made a cake and cookies in my life.

We eventually get to a stopping point inside and join the men outside. Brittany isn't too happy that Nathan is coming. I still don't get it, but there's nothing I can do. He looks super-hot today and even brought a date. He has some scratches and bruises on his arms today. He avoids the question when I asked what happened, saying he's fine. George, the other salesman, is here with his wife and four kids. Yes, four! The youngest, Mason, is three and he's adorable. George's wife, Greta, has been outside with the kids playing in the yard with Ben. He loves all the attention he's getting, fetching his ball and Frisbee and anything else the kids can find to throw for him.

Alex joins the kids playing with Ben and I melt, my heart completely warming at the sight in front of me. I haven't seen Alex interact with children, yet, and seeing him now, I know he will make a fantastic dad someday. He's running and rolling in the grass with them and Ben jumps on his chest licking his face. All the kids laugh, as do most of the adults watching.

We have a few banquet tables set up in rows to

accommodate everyone. Everyone's gathered and fixing plates and chatting with each other. I check to see if anyone needs anything and help make the kid's plates so their parents can relax. I'm sure they don't get much of that. Alex helps me. We sure make a great team.

"I love you," he says and kisses my cheek as we carry the plates to the kids.

"I love you, more."

We make our plates and join our parents who are all seated together along with Brittany, who doesn't seem too pleased that Nathan's completely ignored her the entire evening. Maybe she realizes now how much she likes his attention. Hopefully, it's not too late. I can't help but laugh at her, staring at Nathan and his date, then nudging her.

"Alex, I absolutely adore your girlfriend," Martha says.

"She's pretty great isn't she," he smiles at me.

I find myself blushing. "Thank you, Mrs. Rogan."

"Please, call me Martha, dear." I nod and smile at her.

"Alex, I love your house. Did you design it yourself?" My mother asks.

"Yes, I did. Thank you. I'm hoping Jessa will help me with some decorating. It needs a woman's touch."

"It does, son," his mother adds. "You should take Jessa shopping to fill it up."

"Wow, mom! Tell me how you really feel. I can't even get her to let me buy her clothes without hearing the third degree."

"That's a sign of an independent woman. She's a keeper. Don't let her get away," she says almost in warning.

"That she is and I won't let her get away," he says, taking my hand in his. I look at my mom and she looks like she could cry. I smile at her, a little concerned. Maybe the alcohol's getting to her.

George, his wife and their kids leave shortly after dinner to get the kids bathed and ready for bed. They had a lot of fun with Ben and are dirty and tired by the end. Most of the employees have left except for Nathan. His date has an early work day so she also left shortly after dinner. Brittany is sitting in the corner alone. Nathan walks over and sits with her. She's been getting a bit tipsy, watching him with the new bitch, as Brittany calls her, and it seems she's almost tolerating him now. I see him talking and she's nodding so all seems to be well with them for now.

Alex and I clean up the kitchen and get all the leftovers put away and the dishwasher loaded.

"I think it was a great day. Everyone seemed to enjoy themselves." He jerks his chin toward the window where Brittany and Nathan are sitting. "I think they're even getting along now."

"I think it's been great. It's not over yet. We still need to have dessert." He grabs the cake and tray of cookies.

It's a beautiful night, not too warm to where the mosquitos are attacking us. There's a light breeze blowing the leaves. It's just a perfect night to enjoy with family and friends.

"Jessa, can you go inside and get a knife for the cake?" Alex asks.

"Sure, be right back," I answer, walking inside.

"Thanks, babe," he winks.

When I return, everyone's gathered at the table and excited for cake. I hope it's good. Everyone's looking at me and I'm wondering if I have something in my teeth or a hanging booger.

"Here's the knife," I say, looking at everyone strangely, rubbing my nose to be sure. Everyone focuses on their cake as it's being passed out and I guess I'm just imagining them acting weird. They must all be tipsy. I know I am.

"Baby, have you seen Ben since George left?"

I look around and can't remember seeing him since they'd left.

"Ben," I call. I don't see him. "Ben," I call for him again and whistle and his little chunky self comes running to me from the side of the house.

"Where have you been, you silly boy," I say as he jumps into my lap. I pet him and kiss his head and that's when I see it. I gasp, covering my mouth and look up to Alex, now kneeling beside me, smiling with tears in his eyes. I look around the table and everyone's smiling, too. My mother, Martha and Brittany are all wiping tears from their eyes.

"Jessa, I love you so much. You are my everything. You've helped me get through so much and helped me become the man I now believe you deserve. I want to spend the rest of my life with you. I want to have children with you. I know we weren't each other's first, but I want you to be my *LAST*. I want you to be my wife." He takes the ring off Ben's collar and slips it onto my shaking hand. I'm crying at his beautiful words and the most beautiful ring I've ever seen.

"Will you marry me and spend the rest of your life with me?" I hear gasps and sniffling around me.

"Yes. Of course, I'll marry you. I love you, so much." I'm crying like a baby as he lifts me into his arms and kisses me with such love, such passion. It's the most amazing feeling I've ever felt. True love.

Everyone congratulates us, hugs and kisses each of us. I'm in awe. I can't believe he proposed. I had no idea. All the people that mean the most to me are here to witness this special moment with us.

"I want to thank everyone for coming. It means a lot, to both us, that you could be here," Alex says.

"I want to propose a toast to the happy couple," John, Alex's father, says. "I am truly proud of the man in front of me today and I have no doubt that Alex will be a wonderful husband to my beautiful soon-to-be daughter-in-law. We wish you joy and happiness together and don't wait too long. I want some grandchildren." He raises his glass and pats Alex on the back. Everyone laughs and says, "Cheers."

"Dad, that means so much to me, you saying that. I want to make you proud, not only with the company, but as your son, too," he says with tears in his eyes.

"You have, son."

"I want to say something, as well," my mom says. Oh, lord. I hope she doesn't embarrass me. "Alex, I know we had a rocky start, and I apologize. I see how happy you make Jessa and I couldn't have asked for a better son-in-law. I want you to know, I love you and I'm happy for you both. I also second John's statement on the grandchildren. I'm not getting any younger," she smiles. Everyone laughs. She hugs Alex and then kisses his cheek.

After the women drool over my ring a bit, everyone leaves to give us time to celebrate alone. I even heard the mention of grandchildren again. I'm not ready for that, but don't mind practicing.

As soon as Alex closes the door I jump into his arms, "I love you so much."

"I love you, too". Did I surprise you?"

"You sure did. That was the sweetest proposal. I love that you included Ben."

"I'm so glad. Brittany gave me the idea."

"It was perfect. I can't wait to be your wife."

"I can't wait for that either. Let's go practice on those babies," he says, slapping my ass as we hurry upstairs.

I lay here next to my fiancé. I keep replaying the night's events in my head. The love we shared with each other tonight was like nothing I have ever experienced before. It was like the night he told me he loved me but tonight was so much more. He was so caring, passionate and worshipped me, every single inch of my body. I cried during and after the most mind-blowing orgasms I have ever had.

I can't believe how different my life is. I would have never expected this. When I was a child, this was exactly what I wished for. It may not have happened exactly the way I thought it would, but I have the man of my dreams, a job I love, a beautiful home, and even a dog who I adore. Now, the only thing I'm missing is children. That won't be too far away, but I don't want to share Alex just yet.

We may not have been each other's first but I have no doubt that we are each other's *LAST*.

THE END

ACKNOWLEDGEMENTS

I want to first and foremost thank my family for being so understanding at how much time and effort it took for me to write this story.

Melanie Harlow has also helped me so much since the very beginning of this journey. I've learned so much from her. She is what I consider my mentor, my guardian angel.

Many other authors along the way have also helped answer a ton of questions and have become wonderful friends. Marie Skye, Harloe Rae, Brooklyn Taylor, Brooke May to name a few. I'm sure there are more and I'm drawing a blank. There were times I could have just given up, but these amazing women helped me to keep going and had faith in me when there were times I didn't. I'm so grateful to all of you more than you'll ever know.

If it weren't for my bestie Brittany, one night over several drinks, throwing around ideas and helping me believe that I could really write it, I may have not written this book. I did it, but not without these awesome people. Thank you all so very much! I love you all!

CONNECT WITH ME

Friend me on Facebook

https://www.facebook.com/jl.davisauthor.7

Facebook page

https://www.facebook.com/JL-Davis-Author-151112122039927/

Goodreads

https://www.goodreads.com/book/show/34705355-last

Website

https://jldavisauthor.wixsite.com/web1

Made in the USA
Columbia, SC
03 July 2017